RUBY AND

A Beauty and the Beast Tale

By Ditter Kellen

Published in the United States of America

Ditter Kellen

P.O Box 124

Highland Home, AL. 36041

Chapter One

Ruby Atwood stepped off the plane at the Louis Armstrong International Airport in Kenner Louisiana a little before noon.

She glanced around at the familiar scenery with a heavy heart. Though Louisiana would always be her home, it would never be the same after today.

Trailing off toward baggage claim, Ruby fought the tears that had been threatening since landing. She'd been notified by the New Orleans Criminal Investigative Division that a man resembling Charles Atwood had arrived in the morgue after a shooting at Barone's Gentlemen's Club the night before.

As her father's only living relative besides her nine-year-old brother, Cameron, it was left up to Ruby to identify the body. And she had little doubt that it was her father lying in that morgue. She'd been frantically calling him all night and morning to no avail.

Poor Cam, Ruby thought, grabbing her bag and heading toward the front to hail a cab. *He must be terrified.*

Cameron's mother, Lucy Peters, a known prostitute and heroin addict, had left only days after Cameron's birth, leaving Ruby and her father alone to raise him.

The fact that Cameron hadn't suffered any obvious adverse effects from the drugs his mother had taken during her pregnancy was a miracle in itself.

"Excuse me," a woman murmured, pulling Ruby out of her reflecting. "Do you have change for a dollar?"

Ruby shook her head. Growing up in New Orleans, she knew just about every scam that could be run. And this woman was definitely a con. "I'm sorry, but I don't carry cash."

Without bothering with a thank you, the woman scurried off in search of a new victim.

Ruby made her way outside in search of a cab; the hot Louisiana sun baking the sidewalk with its scorching rays.

Keeping her fingers wrapped tightly around the handle of her bag, she brought her hand up and flagged a taxi that sat along the curb.

The cab driver quickly pulled forward and rolled down the window. "Where to?"

"Southside Medical Center on Canal Street," Ruby returned, climbing into the backseat.

The cab took off with a jolt, darting in and out of the airport traffic like a seasoned NASCAR driver. "Here for a visit or heading home?"

Ruby met the cabbie's gaze in the rearview mirror. "That all depends on what I find when I arrive."

But she knew. Somewhere deep in her heart, she knew that her father would be lying on a cold slab in the basement of that hospital.

Obviously sensing that she didn't feel up to chatting, the cabbie shifted his attention back to the road and the manic drivers in his path.

Ruby turned to stare out the window, a feeling of dread settling in her gut. What was she supposed to do without her father? Moreover, what would Cameron do?

Twenty minutes later, the cab slowed to a stop in front of Southside Medical Center. "That'll be forty-five dollars."

Ruby dug two twenties and a ten out of the pocket of her jeans and handed it over the seat.

"Would you like for me to wait?" The driver looked at her over his shoulder.

Hesitating, she glanced at the hospital's entrance before gripping the door handle, grabbing her bag, and stepping out. "No, thank you. I don't know how long I'll be." She closed the door behind her.

The hospital loomed in front of her, an overwhelming presence of death and gloom. Though most would see it as a beacon of hope, Ruby only saw finality and despair.

A homeless man sat propped against the wall, unwashed and obviously hungry, if the size of his wrists were any indication.

Ruby wondered if he had family somewhere who missed him, or if he was alone in the world with nowhere to go and no one who cared.

She fished out another twenty-dollar bill from her pocket and handed it to him. "Get yourself a hot meal."

His faded brown gaze lifted to meet her own. "God bless you."

Ruby managed a weak smile, activated the sliding doors, and stepped inside.

"May I help you?" an elderly woman asked from behind a small brown desk.

Ruby noticed she wore a volunteer's vest. "I'm looking for the morgue."

The older woman's eyes flickered with compassion. She stood and half turned her frail body toward the hall. "Do you see the elevators?"

At Ruby's nod, she continued, "They will take you to the basement. Once you get off the elevator, take a left, and the morgue will be down on your right."

"Thank you." Ruby trailed off in the direction of the elevators.

She pressed the *down* arrow, waited for the doors to open, and then stepped inside, switching her bag to the other hand.

The elevator lurched downward with a quickness that rolled Ruby's stomach before jerking to a stop in the basement.

Ruby steadied herself while waiting for the doors to open, then stepped into the hall and took a left.

Passing several doors along the way, she finally came to the one that read *Morgue.*

She lifted her hand to knock, noticing that it shook.

The door opened a few moments later, and a balding man wearing a white coat stood in the entrance. "What can I do for you?"

Ruby stared at the mask hanging askew around his neck. "I'm Ruby Atwood. I'm here to identify my — One of your..."

"Yes, of course, Miss Atwood," he interjected, saving her from speaking the words aloud. "Right this way."

Stepping inside, Ruby waited for the door to close, allowing her gaze to scan her surroundings.

Two stainless steel tables sat in the center of the room. A set of matching sinks perched nearby, and large shiny drawers lined the opposite wall.

"I'm Doctor Crowder," the man announced, waving a hand toward the rows of drawers. "You will be doing this alone, then?"

Ruby pinched the bridge of her nose. "There is no one else."

"Very well."

Following him across the room, Ruby stood back as he gripped the handle to one of the drawers and slowly tugged it open. "Are you sure you're ready?"

At Ruby's nod, he gently pulled the sheet down to the man's chest and took a step back.

Fear of what she would see almost took Ruby to her knees. She inched forward until the dead man's face came into view.

"Oh God," she moaned, her hand going to her mouth. Tears sprang to her eyes, instantly spilling over to track down her cheeks. "Daddy…"

Chapter Two

The Beast prowled the halls of his riverside mansion, inconsolable and furious beyond comprehension.

He knew his staff huddled downstairs in fear, but he didn't care. Charles Atwood was dead. The only man alive that could break the curse the Beast had lived with for nearly thirty years.

Born Lincoln Barone, the Beast had been cursed for the sins of his father, Stanford Barone, by Agatha Atwood, Charles Atwood's mother.

According to Agatha, Stanford had seduced her only daughter, Charlotte. After learning that she carried his child, Charlotte had approached Stanford with the news, only to be turned away and told never to contact him again.

Unable to bear the pain of losing him, Charlotte threatened to go to Stanford's equally pregnant wife. Needless to say, Charlotte disappeared that night, and her body was never recovered.

Agatha had gone into a rage, ranting about revenge and voodoo curses.

A week later, a card had arrived on Stanford's doorstep addressed to his unsuspecting pregnant bride. It read, *maledictus.* Latin for *cursed.*

Stanford had chalked it up to the ramblings of a grieving mother, until the day his hideous son screamed his way into the world, and his beautiful young bride closed her eyes forever.

"Stiles!" the Beast roared, spinning toward his darkened bedroom. He could hear the butler's footsteps rushing up the stairs.

"Sir?" Stiles breathed, obviously nervous and out of breath.

Loki, the one hundred-forty-five-pound gray wolf lying near the foot of the bed, growled low in his throat as Stiles came barreling into the room.

Keeping his back to the butler, Lincoln pulled the hood of his cloak over his head, unclenched his teeth, and spoke in a voice more beast than man. "Are you sure Atwood is dead?"

"I-I spoke with the coroner," Stiles stammered. "The daughter has identified him."

The Beast stilled, every muscle in his body taught with tension. "Ruby is here?"

"Y-yes sir. She arrived in town around noon today."

Letting that piece of information sink in, Lincoln moved to the window to stare out at the river beyond. "Call Templeton. I want him here within the hour."

"Right away, sir."

The Beast waited for the door to close behind Stiles before turning to peer down at what was left of the rose encased in glass, resting on his nightstand.

Four more weeks, Lincoln thought, lightly touching the fragile glass, and the curse he'd been born into would forever be his fate.

Stalking across the room to sit on the side of his bed, Lincoln lifted his gaze to the covered mirror in the corner, and a growl similar to Loki's rumbled in his chest. He wouldn't look. He refused to.

The mirror continued to mock him the longer he sat here, calling to him and taunting him with its inhumanity.

With a snarl of surrender, the Beast jumped to his feet, strode across the room, and ripped the covering away from the mirror.

A howl rose up, but he swallowed it back and stared into the eyes of the man he would never be.

He lifted an unsteady hand to his face, afraid to touch it yet unable to stop himself. The feel of the skin beneath his fingers told a different story from the man he saw in the mirror.

But he wasn't a man, he acknowledged, feeling the dusting of hair on his cheeks and nose, the slants to the corners of his eyes, his larger than normal forehead. And his teeth. He didn't even want to think about his teeth. He'd seen less frightening teeth on Loki.

Yet the man staring back at him from the reflection of the mirror had a square jaw, full lips, electric blue eyes, and straight white teeth.

"Blast you, witch!" the Beast snarled, batting the mirror away from him. "I hope the worms feast on you for eternity."

The sound of glass breaking did little to soothe his rage. Even if he never looked into that mirror again, the image of his true form would forever be burned into his brain.

A soft knock on his bedroom door brought Lincoln's head up. "Come."

"I brought you some dinner," Mrs. Tuff announced, opening the door and stepping into the room. She held a large covered tray in her hands.

The Beast barely spared her a glance. "I'm not hungry."

"I'll just leave it right here for you in case you change your mind."

Feeling slightly annoyed that he'd allowed his temper to surface, Lincoln waved the housekeeper forward. "I'll take it."

She hesitated.

"I said, I'll take it!" he snapped, holding out his hand.

Mrs. Tuff scrambled forward, her eyes wide with uncertainty. She handed him the tray.

Lincoln noticed that she wore makeup and her hair appeared different. "Are you going out?"

Clearing her throat, she stared at a place beyond his shoulder, an obvious attempt to avoid looking upon his hideous face. Not that he blamed her.

"Stiles and I are having dinner together in the dining room," she whispered while wringing her hands. "Would you care to join us?"

It was no secret that Stiles and Mrs. Tuff were enamored of each other and had been for years.

A normal person wouldn't have picked up on the subtle looks and touches exchanged when they thought no one was looking, but the Beast wasn't normal. Far from it in fact. His beastly eyes could see as well as his wolf, Loki. If not more so.

"I prefer to eat in my room," was all Lincoln could manage.

Mrs. Tuff continued to stand there, staring over his shoulder. He assumed she waited for him to dismiss her. "Go eat. And be sure to send Templeton to me the moment he arrives."

With a quick nod, the housekeeper scampered from the room as if Loki had suddenly bounded to his feet and came after her.

The Beast glanced in envy at the wolf. Loki had not a care in the world other than his next meal and finding a tree to hike his leg on.

The giant wolf lifted his head and pawed at the floor in front of him. He didn't care about Lincoln's looks or the raspy growl of his voice. Loki loved the Beast unconditionally. And

Lincoln was more than aware that it would be the only love he would ever have.

Chapter Three

Ruby arrived home a little after dark. She paid the driver and climbed from the cab with her bag in hand.

After filling out the proper paperwork at the morgue, she'd spent the next three hours at the police department being questioned by a seasoned detective with a bad attitude.

Detective Richard Hall was the lead investigator assigned to her father's case. He'd informed Ruby that Charles Atwood had been last seen gambling the night before at Barone's Gentlemen's Club on Bourbon Street. He had been shot shortly after leaving the club.

Ruby had also found out that Cameron was at Mrs. Fleming's, the next-door neighbor, where Charles had left him before going out the previous evening.

Mrs. Fleming had often taken care of Ruby after school as well in her younger years, and Ruby trusted her with her life.

Rushing up the steps to her two-story home on Royal Street, Ruby unlocked the door and slipped inside.

Her heart seized as the silence quickly enveloped her. She would never again see her father's smiling face or hear his booming laughter.

Blinking back the tears that threatened once more, Ruby numbly made her way to her bedroom, dropped her bag on the floor, and threw herself across her bed.

Who would want to kill her father? He was the gentlest soul Ruby had ever known.

She rolled to her back to stare up at the ceiling. Why would her father return to gambling after ten years of walking the straight and narrow?

Her stomach abruptly growled, reminding her that she hadn't eaten since the day before. But the thought of food nauseated her.

Slowly rising, she made her way to the bathroom to rinse her overheated face.

Ruby stared at her reflection in the mirror above the sink. Dark circles adorned her red-rimmed eyes—eyes that appeared foreign to her, as if they belonged to someone else.

No matter how much her mind screamed in denial, her father was gone, and life without him would never be the same.

After repeatedly splashing her face with cool water from the sink, Ruby pulled her blonde hair back into a ponytail, took a calming breath, and left the bathroom.

She approached her father's bedroom with trepidation, stopping in front of his door with her hand on the knob.

Not yet, Ruby silently acknowledged, releasing her hold on the knob and turning away. *I'm not ready.*

The thought of going through her father's things, breathing in the smell of his cologne that always permeated his room was more than Ruby could handle at the moment.

She trailed off toward the front door and stepped out onto the small covered porch.

The familiar scents of New Orleans surrounded her in a blanket of comfort as they always did. Lights and sounds merged together to mingle with the laughter and murmuring of voices coming from both sides of the street.

Ruby studied the mass of smiling tourists chattering away as they moved along the sidewalks like ants in search of their next hill.

She shook off her thoughts, melding into the constantly moving throng of people to reach Mrs. Fleming's porch.

Rubbing her sweaty palms along the front of her jeans, Ruby reached up and pressed the doorbell. The door opened a moment later.

"Ruby," Mrs. Fleming crooned, pulling Ruby into a warm hug. "I have been so worried about you. You haven't answered your phone."

Hugging the elderly woman back, Ruby kissed her weathered cheek. "I'm sorry, Mrs. Fleming. I've had a lot going on."

"I know you have, dear." Mrs. Fleming pulled back to gaze into Ruby's eyes. "Cameron is in the TV room watching cartoons. The shooting has been all over the news, so I made sure to avoid those channels. He doesn't know about your father, yet. I figured it would be better coming from you."

Stepping inside and closing the door behind her, Ruby squeezed the old woman's hand. "I can't thank you enough for always being here for us. I don't know what we would have done without you."

"Nonsense. Your grandmother was like a sister to me. We were neighbors for years, until she passed away. It's been nice having you and your brother next door. Agatha would be so proud if she could see you now."

"Ruby!" Cameron cried, rushing around the corner to throw his little arms around her waist. "You're home."

Staring over his head into Mrs. Fleming's eyes, Ruby held him tightly against her. "I'm so happy to see you, Cam."

He pulled back, a huge grin on his face. "How long do you get to stay for?"

Ruby found it hard to speak through her jumbled emotions. "For quite a while. Now, go get your things so we can go home."

Cameron ran off down the hall to gather his belongings, his little body bouncing with excitement.

"If there is anything you need," Mrs. Fleming offered, touching Ruby on the arm, "don't hesitate to ask."

Ruby nodded, not trusting her voice.

The sight of Cameron returning with his bag, saved Ruby from falling into a fit of tears and throwing herself into Mrs. Fleming's arms. "I'm ready."

"Remember what I said," the elderly lady reiterated, opening the door for the siblings. "I'm only a few feet away at all times."

Ruby turned to face her neighbor as Cam bounded down the steps. "Thank you again, Mrs. Fleming."

Quickly catching up to Cam, Ruby unlocked the door to their home and followed him inside.

"Daddy?" Cameron called, dropping his backpack on the floor near the kitchen. He turned to face Ruby. "When's Daddy coming home? He left me at Mrs. Fleming's all night."

Unable to prevent the tears that abruptly flooded her eyes, Ruby shut the door, lowering to her knees in front of him. "I have something to tell you, Cam."

Tilting his head to the side, Cameron's face grew pale with anxiety. "Why are you crying?"

Unable to think of an easy way to say what needed to be said, Ruby inhaled a shaky breath and took hold of her brother's hands. "Daddy isn't coming home, Cam. He's gone to heaven to be with Grandma."

"He died?" Cameron whispered, his eyes growing round in disbelief.

Ruby pulled him forward, embracing him tightly. "Yes. I'm so sorry, Cam."

She could feel his tears against her shoulder as they seeped through the material of her shirt. Her heart shattered all over again.

A fierce protectiveness rose inside Ruby. No matter what happened to her from that moment on, or what sacrifices she would have to make, Cameron would want for nothing. She would take care of him until her last breath.

"You're not going to leave and go back to school are you, Ruby?"

"No, love. I'm not going to leave you. Not ever again."

His little arms tightened around her, telling her how much her words meant to him.

No, Ruby wouldn't return to school. She would stay in New Orleans, take care of Cam, and find the man responsible for killing her father.

Chapter Four

"You wanted to see me?" The sound of Templeton's voice was the only solace the Beast had found since learning of Charles Atwood's death earlier that morning.

Keeping his hood in place, Lincoln turned to face his attorney and most trusted advisor. "I want you to find out who killed Charles Atwood, and then bring him to me."

"Dead or alive?" Templeton murmured without missing a beat.

"It matters not."

Templeton stared at him for long moments. "I can almost guarantee that none of ours were responsible. There would have been no need to kill him. Atwood had already lost everything over the past several months in previous card games. And now we have his home."

Lincoln's eyes narrowed beneath his hood. "His home?"

Templeton reached into his coat pocket and pulled an envelope free. "I have the signed deed right here."

Striding forward, Lincoln plucked the deed from Templeton's grasp, his heart pounding with a modicum of satisfaction. "How did you manage this?"

"It was really quite easy, once he had no money left to bet with. It was his last shot to make it back." Templeton paused. "But of course, he never stood a chance. The game had been rigged just as you specified."

Lincoln stared down at the envelope he held, a calmness seeping into his veins. "I want this filed with the courts as soon as possible."

"Already done," Templeton confessed without blinking. "I took care of it first thing this morning. The house on Royal Street now belongs to you. And it's worth a pretty penny."

"I don't care about the money," the Beast growled, tossing the envelope onto the side table next to the glass-covered rose. "I never have."

Templeton shrugged a bony shoulder. "Be that as it may, Ruby Atwood will have thirty days to pay off the monies owed, since the house has been left to her in Charles's will."

"Pay off?" Lincoln softly bit out. "Explain."

Clearing his throat, Templeton shifted his weight. "That was the stipulation Charles demanded before signing the documents. If he lost the game, he would have thirty days to buy back the deed to his home."

"What?" Lincoln snarled, taking a threatening step forward. "How could you allow him to make stipulations?"

Templeton didn't flinch, just continued to stand there, unmoving. "It was the only way he would sign the document, sir. Besides, Ruby Atwood doesn't have the means to come up with six-hundred-fifty-thousand dollars in the next thirty days. She's a college student, and no more than twenty-years old."

Lincoln's eyes became hooded. "Did you kill Charles Atwood?"

That got a rise out of the otherwise calm attorney. "Of course, not. I'm an attorney, Lincoln, not the Hillside Strangler."

Taking another step forward, Lincoln grasped the edges of his hood and slowly pushed it back away from his beastly face. A flicker of fear entered Templeton's eyes, but it left so fast, Lincoln wondered if he'd imagined it. "The chances of me being anything other than what I am now died with Charles Atwood."

Templeton studied Lincoln's face. "You can't know that for sure."

"My father told me of the curse years ago, Templeton. The only person that had the ability to reverse it was Charles Atwood."

"That can't be true," Templeton stressed, his hands going to his hips. "Charles may have been the only one who could reverse the spell, but he couldn't possibly be the only one who could break it. There has to be another way."

Rage boiled the Beast's blood. He peeled his lips away from his sharp teeth and leaned down close to Templeton's now pale face. "I may as well be asked to raise the dead, you fool! I am to be cursed for the rest of my life."

Templeton backed up a step. "We will figure something out. I—"

"You'll what?" the Beast sneered, turning away and snatching open a drawer to the bedside table. He yanked out a folded scrap of paper that had seen better days and handed it to the now frightened attorney. It had come with the rose beneath that glass. "Read it."

Taking an unsteady breath, Templeton pulled a pair of glasses from his shirt pocket, slipped them onto his hawk-like nose, and unfolded the paper. "It's addressed to the child of Stanford Barone."

The Beast nodded toward the paper. "Go on. Read it."

Templeton ran a hand through his thinning hair and turned the paper toward the light. "*Only true love will set you free, from an innocent it must be. You must learn to love that which you hate, or your thirtieth birthday will seal your fate. When the last petal falls it will be too late.*"

"So, you see," the Beast rumbled, barely able to speak the words, "I am to be this for the remainder of my days."

Templeton appeared uncomfortable. He glanced at the glass housing the nearly bare rose. "Your thirtieth birthday is less than a month away. You are expected to love someone you hate and have that love returned by an innocent in the next twenty-nine days?"

"Exactly."

"How come your father never told me about the riddle?"

Lincoln shrugged a giant shoulder. "Maybe he knew it would do no good."

"Where in the world are you expected to find an innocent in the twenty-first century?" Templeton blurted, apparently still in shock.

The Beast returned his hood to his head. "You're missing the point. Virgin or not, no one could ever love a beast, any more than I could love someone I hate. Finding a grain of salt amidst the sands of the beach would be an easier feat."

"I am sorry, Lincoln."

"I don't want your pity," the Beast snarled, spinning around and stalking back to the window. "I want revenge."

The sound of Templeton's shoes clicking on the floor told Lincoln he'd moved to the side table by the bed. He slid the drawer open, obviously returning the paper to its proper place. "Tell me what you want me to do."

"For starters, I want to own Ruby Atwood."

Templeton remained silent for a moment. "And the boy?"

Lincoln thought about Charles Atwood's son. Though the beast inside him demanded revenge, he knew he'd get no satisfaction from harming a child. He must have some humanity in him after all, he decided. Small as it was. "Leave him be. I may revisit him at a later time. I derive no pleasure from hurting children."

"I'll get right on this." Templeton strode toward the door.

"Templeton?"

"Yes?" the attorney quietly answered.

"See that Ruby doesn't find a way to retain that house. I want to own everything she's ever cared about, right down to her favorite pair of shoes. Do you understand? No matter how small or insignificant you think it is."

"I understand." Templeton opened the door, closing it softly behind him.

Chapter Five

Ruby woke before daylight, her arm half asleep and a dull ache throbbing in her shoulder.

She blinked to clear her vision, slipping her arm free of Cameron's head.

He rolled to his side, murmuring something in his sleep that Ruby couldn't make out.

She kissed his sweet, young face and threw her legs over the side of the bed.

Reality, pain in the butt that she was, slapped Ruby in the face with both hands. Her father was dead…

Stumbling across the room, she carefully opened the door and stepped into the hall. Her father's bedroom loomed ahead, silently beckoning her forward.

She took a shaky breath and moved on legs suddenly gone weak.

The smell of his cologne hit her square in the face as she pushed the door open and breached the threshold of her father's most private space.

"Oh, Daddy," she whispered around the lump in her throat, "Why?"

Ruby stood still for several heartbeats, allowing his scent to seep into her very soul.

An overwhelming feeling of loneliness overcame her, creeping into her bones like a cancer. It wrapped around her heart, wrenching a soft cry from her.

Ruby quickly covered her mouth, afraid she would scream and never stop.

Hot, salty tears rolled down her cheeks to drip off her chin. But she didn't care. Her father was gone and never coming back.

She laid her hand on the top of his dresser and dragged her fingertips along its wooden surface. He'd had that dresser for as long as she could remember.

Turning away, her gaze landed on the unmade king-size bed in the center of the room.

Shoes, a random black sock, and a couple of newspapers were strewn along the floor near the side of the bed.

Ruby trailed over to tidy up the small mess when she noticed a box lodged beneath the bed. She lowered to her knees and tugged it free.

Wiping at the tears with the back of her hand, she carefully removed the lid.

Inside were dozens of photos haphazardly stacked together. And on the top lay a picture of her father standing next to a female version of him.

Ruby blinked to clear her tear-blurred vision and turned the photo over. On the back, in faded blue ink, read; *Charles and Charlotte, ready for senior prom.*

Who was Charlotte? Ruby wondered, laying the picture aside to sift through the box. And why had her father never mentioned her before?

She lifted another photo, this one of her grandmother. Ruby ran her thumb gently over Agatha's face, feeling the loss of her all over again.

"Ruby?" Cameron whimpered from the doorway. "I woke up and you weren't there."

He hesitantly stepped into the room. "I thought you'd left me."

"Oh, Cam, I would never leave you, sweetie. Come here." She set aside the picture she held and opened her arms.

Cameron padded across the carpet and lowered his small body onto her lap. "What are you doing in Daddy's room?"

Ruby kissed the top of his head. "Just looking through some old photos. Are you hungry?"

He nodded against her chest. "Can we make pancakes?"

"We sure can. Go brush your teeth and get dressed. I'll go see what we have in the kitchen."

Watching him go, Ruby felt her heart constrict. It killed her inside to see him hurting, to hear the insecurity in his voice.

She took a fortifying breath, pushing her own emotions aside. Cameron needed her strength, the stability only she could provide.

Ruby returned the photo to the box, replaced the lid and pushed it back underneath her father's bed.

She jumped to her feet and headed toward the kitchen with determined steps. There were many things to be done, and sitting around feeling sorry for herself wasn't one of them.

The doorbell rang just as she passed the foyer.

Ruby glanced at her watch while moving to look through the peephole. Who could possibly be visiting before eight o'clock in the morning?

"May I help you?" Ruby inquired after unlocking the door and pulling it open.

A tall, thin man that looked to be in his early sixties stood on the porch, wearing a black suit and holding a briefcase.

His piercing black eyes quickly assessed her from behind his gold-rimmed glasses. "Are you Ruby Atwood?"

"Yes."

"I am sorry to hear about your father's passing."

"Thank you," Ruby returned. "And you are?"

"My name is Saul Templeton. I represent Mr. Lincoln Barone. May I have a moment of your time?"

The name Barone sounded familiar to Ruby, though she couldn't place where she knew it from. "You're a lawyer?"

"I am Mr. Barone's attorney, yes."

"What's this about?"

"If you would be so kind as to allow me inside, I will show you."

Backing up a step, Ruby pulled the door wider. "Please, come in."

With a brief nod of thanks, the attorney strode past her and marched straight to the kitchen as if he'd been there a hundred times before.

Ruby shut the door and followed suit, surprised to find him already sitting at the bar, opening his briefcase.

He laid some papers out before him.

"Would you mind telling me what this is about?" Ruby questioned again, taking a seat across the bar from him.

Templeton peered at her over the top of his glasses. "I regret to inform you that your father signed over the deed to this house before he died."

Ruby sucked in an astounded breath. "What? He— Why— That's impossible. Daddy would never do something like that."

Sliding a stack of papers across the bar, the attorney pinned her with a hawkish look. "Unfortunately, that is exactly what he did."

"There has to be some kind of mistake."

Templeton abruptly stood. "I'm sorry, Miss Atwood. I assure you there has been no mistake. The terms are very clear. If your father's debt is not paid in full within the next twenty-nine days, the house belongs to Mr. Barone."

Ruby could barely form words, her mind scrambling to absorb the blow she'd just been dealt. "My father's debt? I have no idea what you're talking about."

"His gambling debt, Miss Atwood. I'll leave that copy for you to read over at your convenience, as I understand you have funeral arrangements to make. But don't take too long." With that, he snatched up his briefcase and left the kitchen.

Ruby sat frozen on her stool, staring straight ahead as the sound of his footsteps faded and the front door closed behind him.

She lowered her gaze to the papers the attorney had left on the bar, and her stomach tightened in disbelief. Her father had signed away the house, the only home Ruby had ever known. The home that her grandmother had been born in.

Chapter Six

The Beast lifted the hood of his cloak over his head and made his way down the stairs. "Stiles? Ready the boat. I'll be leaving in five minutes."

Stiles lowered his gaze as he always did in the Beast's presence. "Do you know how long you will be gone?"

Taking an impatient breath, Lincoln strode toward the kitchen, calling over his shoulder as he went. "For as long as it takes."

He entered the kitchen with a flourish, nearly startling Mrs. Tuff out of her apron.

"Goodness, you gave me a scare," the housekeeper gasped, her hand flying to her throat.

She quickly spun around to face the stove, an obvious attempt to avoid looking at him. "What can I do for you, sir?"

"I'm heading across the river. I don't know how long I'll be gone, so don't make a plate for me."

The housekeeper nodded while keeping her back to him. "I'll leave your food in the oven, sir. It should keep it warm for a bit."

Not bothering to answer, Lincoln exited the kitchen through the back door and trailed off toward the boathouse.

Stiles emerged seconds before Lincoln reached the dock. "Would you like for me to go with you, Mr. Barone?"

Lincoln shook his cloak-covered head. "I'll be going alone."

"Very well. May I ask where you're going, sir? In case Templeton calls."

"That's not your business any more than it is his," Lincoln barked, brushing past the butler to enter the boathouse. It annoyed him to be questioned. Especially by the paid staff.

He stepped over into the boat that Stiles had readied for him and gripped the wheel.

Backing out of the boat slip, Lincoln turned the vessel toward the opposite shore, his gaze glued to the lights of the French Quarter.

He thought about the last time he'd seen Ruby Atwood. She couldn't have been more than sixteen years old. He had watched her from the shadows as she'd walked home from her afterschool job at Coleman's Cajun Grill.

The beast inside Lincoln had wanted to snatch her into the alley and claw her pretty face. To destroy her life as her grandmother had destroyed his.

He remembered how she'd walked the sidewalks of the French Quarter as if she owned the entire town, her chin held high and a spring to her step. How she would stop off at Spencer Wright's house on Burgundy Street and stay for an hour before going home.

The Beast ground his teeth at the power of resentment that still burned in his veins. Ruby Atwood had lived a life of love and luxury while Lincoln had hovered in the shadows, alone and angry, unable to attend school or do any of the normal things that teenagers participated in.

He had been ridiculed and mocked as a child, harassed and beaten until he'd lost control and attacked a neighboring bully, hospitalizing the child for several days.

Lincoln's loneliness had eventually turned to resentment, bitterness, and finally…hate.

He shook off his unwanted thoughts and parked the boat near the French Market and Jackson Square.

Tying the craft to a dock, the Beast leapt onto the seawall and dropped lithely to the ground on the other side.

Between the black cloak and the cover of darkness, he slipped unseen into an alley and headed toward Royal Street.

There were very few windows on the side of Ruby's house, only stucco and vines.

The Beast slipped quietly toward the back, flattening himself against the wall. The sound of a splash echoed around him.

Someone's in the pool, he acknowledged, easing up behind a rosebush situated at the corner of the house.

He lowered to his haunches, pushed a cluster of roses aside, and zeroed in on the silhouette of a female gliding along the bottom of the pool.

The female form suddenly surfaced, and Lincoln's breath caught.

There, emerging from the pool, wearing a bright pink bikini was none other than Ruby Atwood.

Lincoln couldn't move. All the breath seemed to freeze in his lungs. He'd never seen anything so perfect in all his life.

She climbed the steps from the pool, water sluicing down her body, her skimpy scrap of a swimsuit clinging to her like a second skin.

The Beast swallowed around a throat gone dry and allowed his gaze to drink its fill.

The swimsuit left little to the imagination, kicking him in the gut with a massive dose of self-loathing. He was lusting after his most hated enemy…Ruby Atwood.

A growl of rage rose in his throat, but he managed to swallow it back. Barely.

He removed his hand from the rosebush, allowing the ruby-red flowers to fall back into place. Even their color reminded him of her name.

Fighting against the desire to look again, Lincoln stood and leaned against the side of the house, sucking in great gulps of air. But no matter how hard he tried to push her from his mind, visions of her stepping from that pool tormented his every thought.

"Ruby?" a small voice called out, pulling the Beast out of his mental anguish.

He lowered himself once more to peer through the rosebush.

A small boy entered his line of sight, carrying a cell phone in his hand.

"Somebody wants to talk to you," the boy announced, handing Ruby the phone.

"Thank you, Cam. I'll be in shortly."

Cameron Atwood, the Beast surmised, watching the boy scamper back inside. *Charles's youngest spawn.*

Ruby lifted the cell to her ear. "Hello?"

Lincoln held completely still, straining to hear the muffled voice coming from the phone, but he was too far away.

"Spencer. Hi."

The beast noticed Ruby's shoulders slightly relax. She absently shook her head, switching the phone to her other ear. "I haven't been home long."

Ruby grew quiet for a moment. "Thank you, Spencer, that means a lot. Okay. I'll see you shortly."

Lincoln remained in the shadows, his gaze glued to Ruby as she laid the cell phone on a chair and returned to the water.

She swam with poise, her strokes sure and strong. And why wouldn't she ooze a level of confidence? the Beast asked himself. Her body was perfection. Unlike his own disfigured form.

The old familiar resentment boiled to the surface, seeping into his veins and tunneling his vision.

The Beast saw nothing but Ruby, her body slicing through the water, her voice echoing inside his head, over and over.

She'd lived a life filled with love, surrounded by family and friends, while Lincoln hid away, an outcast...an unholy abomination.

No more, Lincoln silently swore. No longer would she remain free while he lived out the rest of his days in isolation.

Ruby might not be directly responsible for the curse on Lincoln's head, but Agatha Atwood's blood flowed in her veins. And that was as close to revenge as the Beast would ever get.

Chapter Seven

Ruby emerged from the pool and reached for the dry towel that lay folded on top of a small glass table.

She brought the material to her nose, breathing in the familiar scent of home before stepping into her favorite pair of flip-flops.

A feeling of being watched suddenly came over her.

She slowly lowered the towel and scanned the surrounding area. Her gaze landed on the old rosebush at the corner of the house. *Did it just move?*

Dropping the towel onto the back of a chair, Ruby crept forward, her eyes squinting against the inky black darkness of the alley between her house and the next. "Hello?"

Most of the rosebush dwelled in the shadows, leaving only the front visible.

She lifted a hand, easing forward another inch.

"Ruby?"

Nearly jumping from her skin, Ruby let her hand fall away and spun around. "Spencer, you scared me."

"I didn't mean to." He met her halfway across the yard, wrapping her in the welcoming heat of his arms. "What are you doing out here in the dark?"

Ruby hugged him back. "I thought I heard something. It's so good to see you."

Spencer kissed the top of her head. "It's good to see you too, babe. I'm sorry about your dad."

The mention of her father brought tears to her eyes once more. She snuggled closer, needing the comfort Spencer offered. "I've missed you."

"Not half as much as I missed you." Spencer pulled back enough to gaze into her eyes. "When did you get home?"

"Around noon, yesterday."

Disappointment shadowed his handsome face. "And you're just now seeing me?"

Ruby felt contrite. "It's really the first chance I've had. There's been a lot going on with Daddy's…passing."

"I understand." Spencer ran his fingertips along her cheek. "But I could have helped. That's what boyfriends do, Ruby."

A sound, barely audible, reached Ruby's ears. She turned her head back in the direction of the rosebush.

"What's wrong?" Spencer removed his hand from her face.

"I thought I heard something in the alley."

Pulling away, Spencer strode toward the alley in question. "It's probably just a stray cat," he called over his shoulder.

Ruby quickly caught up to him, staying close behind. "Shouldn't we grab a flashlight? It's black as sin back here."

Spencer rounded the rosebush, pulling a set of keys from his pocket. He fumbled around for a moment until a bright blue LED light appeared in the darkness. "Never leave home without one."

A small animal abruptly scurried across the alley, eliciting a gasp from Ruby.

"Crap," she whispered, stepping in closer to Spencer's side. "Was that a rat?"

A soft laugh escaped him. "Come here."

He gently pulled Ruby into his arms and buried his face against her neck. "I got you."

The smell of his cologne was overpowering, Ruby noticed, turning her face to the side.

She'd been seeing Spencer since the tenth grade. And as much as she cared about him, something always held her back when it came to intimacy.

Spencer had respected Ruby's wishes to wait. Sure, they'd done some kissing and a few things they shouldn't have, but Ruby had always stopped it before it could get out of hand.

She wanted her first time to be perfect, special. Not in the backseat of a car or in some cheap motel room.

Ruby wanted the fairy tale.

Spencer's hands coasted down her back to her hips. He pulled her more firmly against him, pressing his body tightly against her.

Ruby stared into the darkness, wondering why she didn't return his desire, yet somehow relieved that she didn't.

"Spencer..."

He eased back immediately. "I'm sorry, babe. I know my timing sucks. I just can't seem to help myself when I'm around you. Come on, let's get you inside."

Ruby accepted his hand and allowed him to lead her from the alley.

She snagged her towel from the back of the chair, wrapped it around her body, and followed Spencer through the glass sliding doors.

"Make yourself at home," she announced as the door slid shut behind her. "I'll be right back."

Rushing up the stairs to her room, Ruby quickly changed into a pair of jean cutoff shorts and a pink V-neck t-shirt. She ran a brush through her damp hair, pulling it back into a ponytail.

Gazing at herself in the mirror, Ruby somehow felt detached, as if the girl staring back at her were someone else.

Her hazel eyes looked tired, and her normally olive-colored skin appeared pale, clashing with the light-blonde tint of her hair.

Her life had been forever changed over the past couple of days. And no matter how much she might wish it to be so, she couldn't turn back the clock and set things right. Her father was gone and never coming back.

Taking a deep breath of resolve, Ruby turned from her reflection and made her way back downstairs to find Spencer in the kitchen where she'd left him.

"Would you like something to drink?" Ruby inquired on her way to the fridge.

"I'll take a beer if you'll have one with me."

She paused with her fingers on the handle of the refrigerator and glanced over her shoulder. "Some of us haven't turned twenty-one yet."

Spencer grinned. "Since when has that ever stopped you, college girl? You run off to California and get religion?"

Ruby found herself returning his smile. "I guess one wouldn't hurt."

"That's my girl."

"Ruby?" Cameron rushed into the kitchen. "Mrs. Fleming wants to know if I can help her with some chores in the morning. She said she'll pay me twenty dollars."

Poor Cam, Ruby thought, staring into his soft brown eyes. He'd been keeping busy since the news of their father's passing. "Sure. What time does she want you there?"

"She said I can stay the night, so we don't have to wake you up so early."

The thought of spending the night alone in her big, empty house didn't appeal to Ruby, but

Cameron needed the distraction, so she relented. Not to mention, she had to make funeral arrangements, and not having Cam underfoot would make things a tad easier. "Go get your things. And don't forget your toothbrush."

He hurried over and threw his arms around her legs. "I love you, Ruby."

"I love you too, Cam."

Spencer eased up behind her and wrapped his arms around her the second Cameron left the room. "I can stay if you don't want to be alone."

Ruby shook her head. "I appreciate it, Spencer, but I have a lot to do, and I need to be able to think clearly."

"You can't do anything tonight, babe. You can do what needs to be done tomorrow while Cameron's in school. I'll help you."

She glanced down at the beer in her hand before setting it on the bar. "Summer break starts tomorrow. Cameron's out of school for the next ten weeks. Would you be too upset with me if I said my goodnights now?"

As much as she wanted to talk to him about the money owed on the house, Ruby couldn't bring herself to do it. She didn't want his pity. No, she would figure something out on her own.

"Of course, I won't be upset with you. I completely understand, sweetheart. Just know that I'm only a couple of blocks away if you need me for anything."

Ruby turned in his arms and hugged him close. "I know. You've always been there for me."

"That's because I love you."

Pulling back slightly, she met Spencer's gaze. "Do you really?"

"You know I do. What kind of a question is that?"

She glanced away before returning his stare. "It's just that…"

"Just that what?" he prompted, giving her a gentle nudge with his arm.

Stepping out of his embrace, Ruby turned to gaze out the glass sliding door at the light of the pool beyond. "We've been seeing each other since the tenth grade. I'm on my second year in college, and we have yet to go beyond a certain point. I don't expect you to continue to wait on me, Spencer."

"Have you waited for me, Ruby?"

Not surprised by his question, Ruby turned to face him. "You think I've cheated on you?"

"I'm sorry if I sounded accusing," Spencer stated. "I only meant that… Well, I… You're a gorgeous girl, Ruby. I know it can't be easy for you to abstain around all those college guys. Especially for two years."

"I haven't strayed, Spencer. It seems like we have this conversation every time I come home."

Spencer ran a hand through his blond hair. "I know, and my timing couldn't suck more. I'm really sorry, Ruby. About everything. My ignorant questions…your dad. Seriously. Forgive me?"

"There's nothing to forgive." She trailed over to the sliding glass doors. "But I do have a ton to do tonight and funeral arrangements to make. Call you tomorrow?"

Stepping in close, Spencer leaned down and brushed his lips across the corner of Ruby's mouth. "I'll bring you coffee and a beignet around nine o'clock in the morning."

"Sounds good. Goodnight, Spencer."

The hairs on Ruby's arms stood on end as she stood in the kitchen and watched Spencer disappear around the corner of the house.

Her gaze scanned the shadows beyond, the feeling of being watched overcoming her once more.

With a slight shiver, she slid the door closed and locked it behind her.

Chapter Eight

The Beast remained in the shadows of Ruby's backyard long after Spencer Wright's departure.

Lincoln knew all about Spencer Wright. He'd made it his life's mission to know everything there was to know about Ruby and anyone close to her.

Spencer was definitely close to her, Lincoln admitted after silently observing their intimate exchange. If there had been any doubt, it left the moment the blond jock placed his palms on Ruby's bare hips.

A growl rose up at the memory of Ruby in Spencer's arms.

Angry that he'd allowed the little tart to get under his skin, the Beast skirted the shrubs along the privacy fence and headed to the east side of the house.

He stepped onto the central air unit and jumped, his fingers locking onto the railing of the balcony above. The balcony to Ruby's bedroom.

The lights were off in her room. He quietly eased the sliding glass door open and slipped inside.

Her scent hit him full in the face, nearly taking him to his knees with its tantalizing sweetness. He'd never smelled anything so incredible in all his life.

Disgust gripped him at the direction of his thoughts. How could he think of Agatha Atwood's granddaughter in any way other than loathsome?

The sound of the front door closing brought Lincoln out of his detestable musing. He inched back, listening intently as the echo of footsteps entered the kitchen below and traveled to the stairs.

He quickly disappeared onto the balcony, leaving the glass sliding door open an inch in his haste.

The bedroom light abruptly came on, and Ruby appeared in his line of vision. She stopped in front of her dresser, opened the top drawer, and pulled some items free.

Lincoln stood frozen to the spot as she gripped the hem of her T-shirt and lifted it over her head.

She tossed the T-shirt onto her bed and shimmied out of her shorts before pulling a short, white nightgown over her head.

Hatred for her warred with a bone-deep desire to touch her, to smell her hair, to —

What am I doing?

Ruby suddenly stilled, her gaze lifting to the mirror to peer at the very spot where Lincoln stood.

A soft gasp escaped her, and spun around to face the door.

The Beast swiftly sailed over the side of the balcony, landing lithely on his feet. He disappeared into the shadows before she had time to make it to the door.

Berating himself for taking such a risk, he slipped through the back allies of New Orleans, unable to remove the image of Ruby in that white nightgown from his mind.

Was she to be part of his curse? A temptation from the devil himself? How could he want something he despised with a passion that tormented his very soul?

He arrived at the seawall a short time later and dropped silently into his boat.

Starting the engine, he headed toward home.

Stiles met him at the boathouse on his return. "I'll see to the boat, Mr. Barone. Your dinner is in the oven."

Nodding his cloak-covered head, Lincoln strode past him without a word. None were needed. His staff knew better than to question him on his comings and goings.

Foregoing his dinner, Lincoln took the stairs two at a time to his room, nearly tripping over Loki in his haste.

The giant wolf lifted his head and made a whiny sound in the back of his throat. He got to his feet, slinked over to Lincoln's side, and sniffed at his cloak.

"You smell her, don't you?" He patted the wolf's head. "I can still smell her myself."

Jerking the cloak from his shoulders, Lincoln tossed it across the room and moved to the window.

His gaze touched on the lights sparkling across the river. Ruby was out there, amidst those lights, wearing that infuriating, white nightgown.

A howl ripped from his throat before he could stop it, startling the wolf at his feet and triggering Loki's own howl.

Lincoln wasn't sure how long he stood there before he spun away from the window, picked up the overturned mirror, and stood it back up.

A piece of glass fell to the floor where he'd broken it earlier in his rage.

He quickly snatched up the blanket he normally used to cover it, hesitating when he caught sight of his reflection in its surface.

His heart hardened with rage at the man staring back at him.

Unable to stop himself, Lincoln dropped heavily onto the side of his bed and peered helplessly at his reflection.

Had he not been born cursed, his life would have been completely different. He could have had any woman he wanted. Doors of opportunity would have opened for him, and the light would have been his friend.

But he would never know the light. Darkness had become a constant companion since the day he'd arrived screaming into the world.

An image of Ruby swimming in that pool floated through his mind, and he bit back another howl. He should have never went there, never watched her from the shadows like a man starved.

Ruby had to be a witch, he silently seethed, never taking his gaze from his reflection. There was no other explanation for his sudden fascination with her.

The sound of the doorbell ringing reached his ears, yanking him back to reality and the realization that he'd been obsessing over Ruby since he'd seen her in that pool tonight.

Actually, if he were being honest with himself, he'd been obsessing over her since he'd heard of her arrival back in Louisiana.

With a snarl of disgust, he jumped to his feet and tossed the blanket over the mirror.

Moving silently across his room, the Beast listened as Mrs. Tuff answered the front door. "May I help you?"

"I need to see Mr. Barone."

Lincoln's lips peeled back over his teeth at the sound of Ruby's voice.

"At this hour?" Mrs. Tuff questioned nervously.

Ruby immediately shot back. "He can either see me now, or I'll wait out here all night until he emerges in the morning. Either way, I'm not leaving until I speak with him."

"Wait right here," Mrs. Tuff stiffly responded.

Lincoln quickly snatched up his cloak and had it on before the housekeeper reached the top of the stairs.

"I heard," he growled before she had a chance to announce his visitor.

Mrs. Tuff sniffed, staring at a place over his right shoulder. "What would you like me to tell her?"

"Send her to my study."

That brought Mrs. Tuff's gaze to his shadowed face. She squinted into the hood of his cloak, obviously attempting to see his eyes. "I'm sorry, did you say send her in?"

"You heard me. And we are not to be disturbed. No matter what you hear. Do I make myself clear?"

"Y-yes, sir," she stammered, spinning on her heel and fleeing.

"Come, Loki." Lincoln waited on the wolf to follow him out and then strode across the hall to disappear into his study.

He rounded his desk, reached back to switch on a lamp behind him, and took a seat.

The light coming from behind him would ensure that he saw her face without her having the luxury of seeing his.

"Down, Loki."

The giant wolf immediately trotted around the desk to lie at Lincoln's feet.

Footsteps on the stairs sent Loki growling.

"Easy, boy. Stay."

The vicious growling eased up some but didn't stop all together.

Pulling the hood down low over his face, Lincoln snagged a pair of gloves from the desk drawer and slipped them on.

He leaned back in his chair to wait.

Chapter Nine

Ruby couldn't believe she was actually in Lincoln Barone's mansion.

Though she'd never seen him before, she knew he was a very powerful man in Louisiana. Not only did he own several reputable shipping companies, but Barone's Gentleman's Club also belonged to him. And Barone's happened to be the biggest, busiest high-end club in New Orleans.

"He'll see you in his study," the housekeeper announced, descending the stairs. "It's the first door on your right at the top of the stairs." With that, she disappeared around a corner, leaving Ruby to her own devices.

Glancing around nervously, Ruby rested her hand on the banister and slowly took the stairs to the top.

No sounds could be heard in the massive house. Not a television, radio, or voices of any kind.

Creepy, Ruby thought, taking in the intricate designs along the banister.

Pictures adorned the walls leading up to the second floor. Some were paintings and some portraits. Most were of a beautiful dark-haired woman with electric blue eyes. Ruby had never seen anyone with eyes so blue.

Others portrayed a handsome man at different stages in his life, smiling and holding onto the blue-eyed woman.

They must not have had children, Ruby concluded, noticing there were no kids in any of the photos. It also didn't escape her that the blue-eyed woman wasn't in the more recent pictures of the man.

Ruby stepped onto the second floor and hesitantly made her way to the first door on the right.

What she saw when she entered the room momentarily stunned her. She couldn't seem to find her voice.

Someone sat behind a big cherrywood desk, wearing a cloak with the hood pulled low over their face. That was strange in itself, but nothing prepared her for the massive animal lying beneath the desk, showing its teeth and growling deep in its throat.

"Is that a timber wolf?" Ruby choked out, afraid to move.

"Enough, Loki!" the cloaked man snapped.

Rooted to the spot inside the door, Ruby stared at the hooded figure for several heartbeats before switching her gaze back to the beast known as Loki. "He... Will it... Is he going to—"

"Sit down, Miss Atwood, and don't make any sudden movements."

Ruby backed up a step. "I'll just come back at a later time."

"Sit!" the man practically roared, scaring Ruby into the chair in front of the desk.

Her heart pounded so hard she was sure that Loki would hear it and rip the beating organ clean from her chest.

"How do you know my name?" Ruby whispered, hating the fear that resonated in her voice.

The hooded man ignored her question, nodding instead to the papers she carried in her hand. "Is that the deed to your house?"

Ruby's mouth dropped open. She laid the papers on his desk and sucked in great gulps of precious oxygen. "It is. How did you —"

"I assure you, the documents are legal, Miss Atwood."

"I'm sure they are," Ruby shot back, her voice gaining strength. "That's not why I've come."

He merely sat there, still as a stone, watching her from beneath that dark hood.

Clearing her throat, Ruby glanced at the timber wolf beneath the desk and shifted in her seat. "I read over the papers, Mr. Barone. I'm assuming you're Mr. Barone?"

At his slight nod, she continued. "I understand that it's legal. I'm here to ask you if we can work out some kind of payment arrangement. I can't lose my home. It's been in my family for years."

"Your father should have thought of that before he gambled it away, Miss Atwood. He obviously didn't care how many years it had been in the family."

Ruby swallowed hard. The raspy growl of the man's voice sent chills up her spine.

She would give anything to be able to see his face, to look him in the eye as she pleaded with him. "I'm aware of that, sir. But you have to understand, Daddy was an addict. Gambling was his weakness. Please don't make my little brother and I have to suffer any more than we already have."

"He made the deal, Ruby. A debt is a debt."

The use of her first name caught Ruby off guard. "H-how…?" She swallowed and tried again. "Have we met before?"

"No. But I know who you are. You're Charles Atwood's daughter. Agatha Atwood's granddaughter."

A strange foreboding came over Ruby. The tone of Barone's voice indicated anger, resentment…malice. But why would it be directed at her? She'd never done anything to him. In fact, he held all the cards as she saw it.

She inhaled a fortifying breath and tried again. "Look, Mr. Barone. All I'm asking for is a bit more time. I feel certain that if you would extend the thirty days—"

"There will be no extension," he interrupted, his voice brooking no argument.

Anger reared its ugly head. Ruby had always battled with her unpredictable temper, and now was no exception. "So, you're going to take our home, just like that?"

She suddenly stood, snatching up the papers with jerky movements. The wolf growling beneath the desk barely penetrated her rage-filled mind. "We'll see about that. You can sit in your creepy mansion, dressed like the Grim Reaper with your scary wolf all you want! But I won't let you intimidate me. I'll have your money to you by the due date. You won't get my house, you freak!"

Spinning on her heel, Ruby turned to go.

But his next words stopped her. "We may be able to work something out."

Ruby stopped in the doorway, her back still to him. "And what might that be?"

"You spend the remainder of the month with me."

Certain she'd heard him wrong, Ruby slowly turned to face him. "Pardon?"

"You heard me. You belong to me for one month, to do with as I please. Not only will the house remain yours, but the money your father lost, the six-hundred-fifty-thousand will be returned to you as well."

Ruby's mouth opened and closed. She blinked a couple of times and stared at him in disbelief. "You want me to sell myself to you?"

"Call it what you will, Miss Atwood. I believe it's a reasonable offer. One month with me, for the money and the house. That's well over a million dollars."

"Money that was mine to begin with!" Ruby snapped, shocked and beyond livid. "You can take your deal and shove it up your arrogant behind, Mr. Barone. I may be a lot of things, but cheap sure isn't one of them."

With that, she stalked from the room. She didn't slow until she reached the ferry that would take her back across the river to the French Quarters.

"I'm sorry, ma'am. The ferry closed ten minutes ago," a tall, lanky man with thinning hair informed her.

Ruby sighed in irritation. "Can you make an exception this once? I'll pay extra."

"I wish I could, but unfortunately everything we do is monitored."

Glancing around the shoreline, Ruby pulled her cell phone from her pocket and called for a cab.

After rattling off the address, she returned the phone to her jeans pocket and glanced up the hill to Lincoln Barone's house. A lone figure stood in the upstairs window.

It suddenly moved, disappearing from view like a phantom.

Ruby shivered and took a seat on a nearby bench to wait on her cab to show, thoughts of her conversation with Barone playing through her mind.

He wanted to own her.

The sheer arrogance of the man astounded her. But his audacity is what took the cake.

What kind of a man would make such a demand?

A very rich one, Ruby silently acknowledged with a frown. *A man with more money than sense.*

The ferry captain finished locking up for the night and trailed over to where Ruby sat. "I live just about a mile inland. You're welcome to walk with me. We can call you a cab once we reach my place."

There was something about the man Ruby didn't trust. Maybe it was the close set of his beady eyes, or the way his gaze remained glued to her chest when he spoke.

Ruby pasted on a brave smile. "Thank you, but my cab should be here any minute."

"It's not safe to sit out here alone in the dark," he persisted.

Looking him square in the eyes, Ruby lied. "I have a weapon. Like I said, I'll be fine."

He glanced down toward her pockets before shrugging. "Suit yourself. But don't say I didn't warn you."

"I appreciate the offer," Ruby responded with a calmness she didn't feel, "but I'll be fine."

More than a little relieved to see him stride off up the hill, Ruby felt her shoulders relax.

She got to her feet and glanced at her watch. It had been fifteen minutes since she'd called for a cab.

Ruby began to pace along the river's edge, her gaze scanning the trees for any sign of movement, when two men stepped from the shadows and split up, moving to either side of her.

Taking a step back, Ruby let her gaze touch on every possible route of escape, her mind freezing up in terror. "Stay back!"

"Don't run, sweetheart," one of the men taunted. "We just wanna talk."

Ruby spun on her heel and darted to the right, running with every ounce of strength she had.

She was abruptly slammed into from behind. Her feet flew out from under her, and she sailed through the air with her hands out in front of her.

The weight of her attacker landed on her back, knocking the wind from her lungs with a force that nearly rendered her unconscious.

Agony sliced through her body, taking what little breath she had left.

A hand wrapped around her ponytail, jerking her head painfully to the side. "What do we have here?"

"Leave me alone," Ruby croaked, barely able to get the words out through her chattering teeth.

"Oh, she's a feisty one, Lester."

The one known as Lester shifted his weight, his knee digging into her back.

Ruby went wild, kicking and clawing with every ounce of strength she possessed, to no avail.

"I like my women wild," Lester sneered, his breath fanning the side of her face.

Tears of terror sprang to Ruby's eyes. No matter how hard she fought, she couldn't free herself from her assailant's hold.

A howl split the night, followed by a snarl and the most vicious growl Ruby had ever heard.

Lester was suddenly yanked from her back and tossed to the side as if he weighed nothing.

Ruby lifted her head in time to see a robed figure grip her attacker by the collar and snatch him to his feet.

Loki sailed through the air, slamming into her assailant's partner. They rolled down the hill in a tangle of snarling arms and limbs.

The screams coming from the man in Loki's grasp would haunt Ruby for the rest of her life. But nothing prepared her for the power the robed figure unleashed on Lester.

Bones crunched with every forceful blow of Barone's fist to the man's face. And Ruby knew it to be Barone as surely as she knew that no man alive possessed the kind of strength he exhibited in that moment.

She staggered to her knees, unable to take her gaze from the brutal scene before her.

Barone's hood slipped off, and the moon's silver glow flashed off the sharp points of his teeth.

Ruby stumbled back in horror, a scream lodging in her throat.

The trees began to spin around her. She blindly reached out, grasping for something, anything to keep from falling. "Help me," she slurred as her world turned black.

Chapter Ten

Rage consumed the Beast as he ripped the shirt off the guy he held in front of him, and roared in his face. Visions of him attacking Ruby stormed through Lincoln's mind.

The sleazy piece of scum screamed like a woman, both of his hands coming up to grip the Beast's wrists. "P-please…"

Headlights suddenly flashed across Lincoln's face, jerking him out of his murderous state.

He tossed the man into the river without batting an eye.

"Loki, come!"

The massive wolf lifted his head, releasing the man beneath him.

"Come!" the Beast snarled once more.

His gaze then shifted to the man huddled on his side at Loki's feet.

Pointing toward the place where he'd tossed Ruby's assailant, the Beast peeled his lips back to show his teeth. "Swim."

The downed man scrambled toward the water, his shirt torn to shreds, and his arms and hands bleeding profusely.

"If I see your face around here again, I will kill you with my bare hands."

A choked sound came from the man, but he didn't slow. He fell into the river with a splash, swimming toward his partner like the devil himself were after him.

Lincoln quickly scooped Ruby up into his arms, noticing her unconscious state.

He strode toward the house, trusting that Loki would follow. Which he did.

"I need warm water, bandages, and towels," Lincoln barked, bursting through the front door like a bull in a china shop.

Mrs. Tuff rounded the corner, her hand flying to her throat.

It took a moment for Lincoln to realize that his hood had come off.

Storming up the stairs, he called over his shoulder. "Now, Mrs. Tuff!"

Lincoln couldn't stop looking at Ruby's face. Her long, dark lashes resting against her now pale cheeks gave her an ethereal appearance. She had to be the most perfect creature he'd ever seen.

Resentment quickly overcame him, forcing him to look away from her beautiful face.

He told himself that he'd come to her rescue out of duty. She was, after all, going to belong to him for a month. And he couldn't have her bloodied and bruised.

He arranged her gently on his bed, replaced his hood, and brushed a few strands of hair from her face. The rest of her hair, he noticed, was pulled back into a ponytail.

Leaning in close, Lincoln carefully wrapped his fingers around the bound locks and brought it to his nose.

His eyes slid shut the second her floral scent invaded his senses.

What was it about her that kicked him in the gut when she was near? Sure, she was beautiful, but she was an Atwood, spawned from the very evil responsible for his curse.

Releasing her hair, he jumped back when Mrs. Tuff rushed into the room.

"Here are the things you asked for."

He noticed that she'd gone back to looking over his shoulder, even though his hood had been replaced. "Set them on the bedside table, and then get out."

With a stiff nod, Mrs. Tuff did as he asked, pulling the door shut behind her as she left.

But not before Lincoln saw the disapproving look in her eyes. Well, she could kiss his cursed behind. When he wanted her opinion, he would ask for it.

With infinite care, he picked up a washcloth, dipped it in the warm water, and began removing the mud from Ruby's face.

She softly moaned, turning her face toward him, but her eyes remained closed.

Lincoln managed to get most of the grime from her arms without waking her. He checked her head for a possible concussion but found no injuries there.

Bruises marred her skin below her elbows, and a cut on her hand bled onto the sheets of his bed.

He carefully cleansed the wound and wrapped it with gauze, satisfied that she didn't need stitches.

She suddenly moaned, a soft sound full of pain and fear.

Lincoln stepped back, pulled his hood low, and waited for her eyes to open.

He didn't have long to wait.

Ruby sucked in a breath and scrambled back against his headboard. Her gaze darted around the room, undoubtedly looking for a way of escape. "Where am I?"

"In my room," the Beast rumbled, remaining a few feet from the bed. "You were attacked down by the river. Do you not remember?"

He saw the moment realization dawned.

Her eyes grew round, and she pressed herself more tightly against the headboard. "Are they dead?"

"I let them live. But I doubt they will return. Are you hurt anywhere besides the obvious places?"

She shook her head, her hand automatically going to her ribs.

The Beast took a step forward and batted her hand aside. "Let me see."

"Don't touch me!" Ruby cried, fear apparent in her hazel-colored eyes.

Anger sparked again. "I saved your life, you ungrateful twit!"

"Twit?" Ruby gasped, slapping at his hovering hand.

She jumped from the bed, nearly toppling at his feet. Her hand flew to her head, and she stumbled back against the bedside table.

"Lie back down before you hurt yourself even more," Lincoln demanded, taking hold of her arm to steady her. "I'm not going to harm you."

Though suspicion still lurked in her eyes, she did as she was told.

Lincoln watched her fumble around in the pocket of her jeans and pull a cell phone free.

After pressing a few buttons, she brought the phone to her ear.

The one-sided conversation told him that she'd called a cab, which meant she would be leaving soon.

She returned the cell to her pocket and lifted her leery gaze. "What's with the Quasimodo getup?"

Obviously, she didn't recall seeing his face in the heat of the fight by the river.

He sidestepped the question, instead answering with one of his own. "How do you propose to come up with the money to save your house?"

Her eyes flashed in resentment. "That's none of your business."

"Everything you do is my business," he shot back. "Besides, think of your brother. What will he do when you lose your home? How do you plan on feeding him, clothing him?"

Throwing her feet back to the floor, Ruby awkwardly stood and limped her way to the door. "You let me worry about my family. The house is still mine for the next twenty-nine days. I suggest you stay away from us."

Lincoln glanced at the clock on the wall. It was now after midnight. "Twenty-eight days."

"Whatever."

Chapter Eleven

Ruby took the stairs to the bottom floor, her chin held high in defiance. If that freak thought to blackmail her into submitting to him, he was sorely mistaken.

He had to be at least fifty years old if the photos on the wall were any indication. That was a lot older than Ruby's mere twenty years of age.

The housekeeper met Ruby at the foot of the stairs. "Do you need me to call you a cab?"

Ruby noticed the woman had kind eyes. "I have one on the way. But thank you."

"Don't let Mr. Barone frighten you too much. He's more bark than he is bite. Well, most of the time."

Bark...bite. Something teetered at the edge of Ruby's conscience. Something she couldn't quite grab onto. She quickly shook it off and gave the housekeeper a reassuring smile. "I'm not scared of him. Bullies only have power if you give it to them."

The housekeeper appeared nervous, as if afraid Ruby's comment would be overheard. "You are welcome to wait in the sitting room until your cab arrives. It can be very dangerous on this side of the river at night."

Don't I know it, Ruby thought, opening the front door and stepping onto the porch. "I'll take my chances out here with the bugs. But I appreciate the offer."

Once the door closed behind her, Ruby wandered along the front of the house and took a seat on a beautiful wrought iron bench. The light from the porch glowed enough to show the intricate design woven along the seat back.

She squinted through the fog, watching the lights from the city twinkle across the river beyond. New Orleans had to be the busiest, most soulful place Ruby had ever known.

Though she loved California and had grown accustom to its beauty and diversity while attending college there, it would never be home.

Glancing at her watch, Ruby realized it was closing in on one in the morning. What had she been thinking going to Barone's house after dark?

Lights from a car suddenly swung up the hill, moving through the fog like the eyes of a demon.

Ruby got to her feet, glancing up at the window above her on the second story. There, gazing down upon her, the eerie glow of a lamp behind him, stood the cloak-covered Lincoln Barone.

She quickly looked away, unable to bear his image a second longer.

What was it about him that made her so uneasy? Aside from the creepy hood covering his head, he was just a man. And an older man at that. It wasn't as if he'd been accused of murder or spent time behind bars for any crimes that Ruby knew of.

"Where to?" the cabbie asked, rolling down his window.

Ruby gave him her address and climbed into the welcoming safety of the back seat.

"That's the Barone mansion, isn't it?" The driver nodded toward the mansion while easing forward along the circular drive.

Ruby glanced back at the house, her gaze immediately going to the window on the second floor only to find it empty. "It's more like a crypt, but yes."

The rest of the ride home was spent in silence. Ruby had never been so glad to see her house as she was stepping out of that cab. She paid the driver and jogged up her steps.

Home, she silently acknowledged, unlocking the door and stepping inside. *But not for long if I don't figure out a way to pay off Daddy's debt.*

* * * *

A pounding on the door jerked Ruby out of her sleepy state.

She quickly sat up in bed, certain that she was dreaming.

The pounding sounded again, only louder this time.

Ruby sailed from the bed, glancing at the clock on her nightstand. It was just after eight in the morning.

Grabbing a robe, she hurried through the house to the front door, disengaged the locks, and jerked it open. "Mrs. Fleming?"

The elderly neighbor stood on the top step, tears in her faded brown eyes. "It's Cameron. He's been in an accident."

"What?" Ruby whispered, the breath leaving her lungs in a rush. "What are you talking about?"

Mrs. Fleming pushed past a numb Ruby and rushed inside. "He went out this morning to grab us some donuts and stepped off the curb in front of an oncoming car. Hurry, you must get dressed!"

Ruby stood rooted to the spot, her brain unable to process what she'd just heard. "Is he— What did— Is he okay?"

"I don't know!" Mrs. Fleming cried. "The manager of the café he was in front of called an ambulance. When he didn't come right back, I went to check on him and was told what had happened. He was taken to the Southside Medical Center on Canal Street."

"That's a trauma center," Ruby breathed, snapping out of her frozen state.

She ran to her bedroom and changed into the first thing she could find in her haste to get dressed.

Mrs. Fleming appeared in the doorway of Ruby's bedroom as she was lacing up her running shoes. "I am so sorry, Ruby. This is all my fault."

"Don't you blame yourself, Mrs. Fleming. You had no way of knowing this would happen."

Grabbing her cell phone and wallet, Ruby sailed past the elderly neighbor and hurried toward the front door. "I'll call you as soon as I hear anything."

"Shouldn't you get a cab?" Mrs. Fleming called out, attempting to catch up.

Ruby glanced back, shaking her head as she bounded down the steps. "There's no time. It'll take them twenty minutes to arrive. I can be there in less time than that."

"Be careful!" Mrs. Fleming's voice could barely be heard over the thundering of Ruby's heart.

Ruby had one thing on the brain as she darted across the street and shot through the closest ally. *Cameron...*

Ten minutes later, an out of breath Ruby flew through the automatic doors of the emergency entrance of Southside Medical Center. She could barely get the words out past her labored breathing. "Cameron Atwood."

A nurse looked up from a chart she held. "Are you okay, miss?"

"My little brother was brought in this morning," Ruby gasped, attempting to slow her breathing. "He was hit by a car."

"And you are?"

"Atwood. Ruby Atwood. My brother's name is Cameron."

"Come with me. I believe your brother is still in surgery."

Ruby's heart seized up in her chest. "Surgery? Is he going to be okay?"

"I don't know," the nurse answered honestly, pity swimming in her kind eyes, "but we'll see what we can find out."

Grateful for the nurse's help yet terrified of what she would learn, Ruby followed her to the nurses' station.

"Where's the chart on the car accident victim?"

Glancing at Ruby apologetically, the nurse cleared her throat before returning her gaze back to a dark-haired woman sitting in front of a computer screen. "This is the child's sister."

The brunette looked up from her task of typing. "I'll need to get some information from you."

Ruby stepped forward, anxiety tightening her gut. "Can you tell me how Cameron is, please?"

"He's still in surgery. But I can get an update for you."

"Thank you. I really appreciate that" — Ruby glanced at the woman's nametag — "Karla."

Pulling some papers from a drawer, Karla attached them to a clipboard and handed them to Ruby. "Would you mind filling these out for me while I check on your brother?"

Ruby accepted the clipboard and set it on the counter to fill in the designated information. Ten minutes later, she signed her name on the bottom line and turned to face Karla coming from the elevator. "How is he?"

"Your brother suffered a head injury as well as a broken femur that punctured his femoral artery. He's lost a lot of blood, but they are doing everything they can for him. We'll update you with more information as it comes in."

The floor tilted beneath Ruby's feet. "But he's going to live?"

"All I can tell you is that we have the finest physicians in the state working on him. He's in the best hands he could possibly be in."

Ruby nodded, not trusting her voice. It took her a second to gather the courage to speak. "Can you tell me where the chapel is located?"

Karla's expression softened. "I'll walk you there."

Chapter Twelve

Ruby thanked Karla for her help and then entered the chapel on wooden legs. Cameron was in surgery, fighting for his life.

Kneeling at the altar, Ruby allowed the tears to fall freely from her eyes. She prayed like she'd never prayed before. Yet no matter how much she begged for God to spare Cameron's life, the fear that he wouldn't hear her far outweighed her faith.

Unsure of how long she remained on her knees, Ruby eventually pushed to her feet and stumbled from the chapel without any closure.

She wiped at her eyes with the backs of her hands and made her way down the corridor to the counter where she'd first met Karla. "Excuse me?"

Karla looked up from what she worked on. "Hi. I was just about to come get you. Your brother made it through the surgery."

Relief nearly buckled Ruby's knees. "May I see him now?"

"Not yet," Karla gently informed her. "He's being moved to the ICU recovery room. They'll let you know as soon as it's okay to go in."

"How long will that take?"

Karla shook her head. "It's hard to say. But you will be the first to know the second we find out anything."

Clearing her throat, Karla continued, "I know this is not a good time, but the insurance information you gave us has been declined. Are you certain you wrote it down correctly?"

Ruby frowned and opened her wallet. She pulled her insurance card free and handed it to Karla. "We're both on the same policy. I've never had trouble with it before."

"Give me a minute." Karla picked up a phone. "I'll see what I can find out."

Ruby nodded, resting her elbows on the counter as Karla dialed the number on the back of the insurance card. She listened to the pretty brunette rattle off some numbers, along with her brother's name.

"Are you sure?" Karla pinched the bridge of her nose. "Yes, thank you."

Hanging up the phone, Karla handed Ruby the insurance card. "I'm sorry, Miss Atwood. The policy was terminated for nonpayment two months ago."

Ruby's vision grew tunneled. Her mind couldn't comprehend Karla's words. She stared at the dark-haired nurse for long moments, unable to grasp the reality of what was happening. "He has no insurance? Nothing?"

"I'm afraid not," Karla responded in a quiet voice. "You'll need to call a social worker to see what options they have available for you. Would you like their number?"

Ruby merely nodded, unable to find her voice.

Karla grabbed a card near her computer and gave it to Ruby. "Her name is Lisa Davis. She should be able to help you. In the meantime, if you take the elevator to the third floor, the intensive care waiting room is just across the hall as you emerge. Someone will come get you as soon as your brother can be seen."

"Thank you," Ruby numbly responded. "I appreciate all your help."

Karla reached up and touched her on the hand. "Is there anyone I can call for you? Any family or friends?"

Ruby shook her head. "Cameron is the only family I have left." Her mind drifted to the morgue in the basement, where her father's body still lay in refrigeration.

"Are you going to be all right?"

Ruby pasted on a small smile and met the nurse's gaze. "I'll be fine."

Trailing off toward the elevator, Ruby pressed the *Up* button, waited for the door to open, and stepped inside. She fished out her cell and dialed the number on the card.

A feminine voice came over the line. "This is Lisa Davis."

"Hi, Miss Davis. My name is Ruby Atwood. My brother was in an accident and he's in ICU at Southside Medical Center. Our insurance has lapsed, and I was told to call you."

There was a brief hesitation. "I'm in the hospital now, Ruby. Where are you?"

"On the third floor at the waiting area." The elevator door dinged, and Ruby stepped off in front of the ICU waiting room.

"I'll be right there."

Ruby thanked her and ended the call.

The waiting room was thankfully empty as Ruby solemnly entered. She gazed around at the empty chairs and then decided on standing.

Cameron had no insurance. Ruby couldn't wrap her mind around the fact that her father had allowed it to lapse. How was she going to pay for her brother's care? Between his surgery and the ICU stay, the bills would be astronomical.

Another thought struck her as she stood there in a daze. She had no money for her father's funeral either.

"Miss Atwood?"

Ruby looked up in time to see a pretty blonde woman step into the room, wearing a gray pantsuit and holding a briefcase. "Ruby. Please call me Ruby."

"Very well, Ruby. My name is Lisa Davis." She extended her hand.

Accepting Lisa's outstretched palm, Ruby attempted to smile through the tears that threatened. "Thank you for seeing me."

"Let's have a seat," Lisa suggested, nodding toward a set of chairs across the room, "and see what we can do to help you."

Ruby sat, her body angled toward the social worker's chair. She blurted the first thing that entered her mind. "We no longer have insurance."

Lisa listened with rapt attention as Ruby explained her situation. "I'm sorry about your brother. What about your parents?"

"Our father died a few days ago, and Cameron's mother gave up her parental rights when Cam was a baby. She hasn't been seen since."

"I see." Lisa opened her briefcase and pulled some papers free. "So, the child has no legal guardian?"

Ruby blinked. "Me. He has me."

"I understand that you are Cameron's sister, Ruby. But do you have legal guardianship of him?"

"Legal, as in...?"

Lisa didn't hesitate. "As in signed by a judge."

"Well, no," Ruby answered, anxiety evident in her voice. "Our father just recently passed away. We haven't even buried him yet."

Compassion shone from the social worker's eyes. "I'm truly sorry for your loss, Ruby. But Cameron's needs must be my immediate focus. And without legal custody of him, your signature won't get him the help he so desperately needs."

"What are you saying?"

Lisa laid her palm over Ruby's trembling hand. "The Department of Children and Families will need to be notified."

"No!" Ruby rushed out, snatching her hand away from the social worker's hold and jumping to her feet. "You can't do that. I'll go to the courts and get whatever legal documents you require. Please don't call DCF."

Lisa stood as well. "Your brother needs medical care, Ruby. And without insurance, he'll require help from the state."

The tears Ruby fought so hard to hold back spilled forth to slip down her cheeks. "Will they take him from me?"

"I doubt it," Lisa assured her, reaching up to lightly squeeze Ruby's arm. "Hopefully, they can help you do what needs to be done to acquire parental custody. But you'll need to do something quick. He'll continue to accrue medical bills with every passing hour."

Taking a deep breath, the social worker gave Ruby one last pitying look. "You have my card. Call me if you have any more questions."

Ruby watched her go through a haze of salty tears. She dropped heavily back into her chair, unable to stop the choking sound from slipping from her throat. How much more was she expected to endure before she broke?

So much had happened to her over the last few days. She'd lost her father, her brother lay in ICU, barely hanging onto life. Her family home would no longer belong to her if she didn't come up with six-hundred-fifty-thousand dollars in the next twenty-eight days, and now she ran the risk of losing Cameron to the system.

"Miss Atwood?" a soft voice called from the doorway.

Ruby jerked her head up, furiously swiping at her tearstained cheeks. "Yes?"

"You may go in and see your brother now. He's stable but still in critical condition, so you'll need to make it brief."

Ruby pushed to her feet and followed the nurse down the hall to the left. "Can you tell me about his injuries?"

The nurse sent her a reassuring smile. "The doctor will be in shortly to fill you in on his condition."

Stopping in front of a set of open double doors, the nurse sanitized her hands, and then strode through.

Ruby followed the nurses lead, moving to the bottle hanging from the wall. She rested her palm underneath and caught the alcohol-scented gel that quickly dispensed.

After assuring herself that her hands were germ free, Ruby trailed after the nurse into an ice-cold room full of equipment, cords, and beeping sounds.

Cameron lay in the center of it all, his face pale as a ghost's, a bandage on his head, his leg in a cast, and a blue tube coming from his mouth.

"It's a breathing tube," the nurse informed her. "We'll need to be sure he can breathe on his own before it can be removed."

A short, thin man stepped into the room, wearing a white coat and holding a clipboard in his hand. The nametag on his right breast coat pocket, read *DR. CHEN.*

"Are you the sister?" the doctor asked, glancing up over the top of his wire-rimmed glasses.

"I am. Is he going to be all right?"

Doctor Chen moved to the side of the bed and began scribbling something in Cameron's chart. "Your brother suffered extensive injuries, including a severe concussion that resulted in a brain bleed. We managed to get the bleeding stopped, but we're keeping an eye on it to be sure. We had to remove a small piece of his skull to release the pressure from his brain."

Laying the chart on the foot of Cameron's bed, the doctor met Ruby's gaze. "He's lost a lot of blood. His femoral artery was severed due to the break in his femur. We were able to repair it in time before he bled out. It's going to be touch and go for a few days, but he's young and strong. I believe he'll pull through."

"Thank you," Ruby whispered around the lump in her throat. "Thank you so much."

Chapter Thirteen

The Beast stared out the window of his second-story bedroom, gazing at the lights across the river. It had been two days since Ruby's midnight visit to his home. Two days since he'd slept...

"Templeton is here to see you," Mrs. Tuff announced from the open doorway.

Keeping his back to her, the Beast answered in a monotone voice. "Send him in."

The rustling of clothes along with the sound of footsteps could be heard coming up the stairs. They stopped just inside Lincoln's bedroom.

"Any news?" the Beast rasped, his gaze still locked on the lights of the city in the distance.

Templeton made a sound in the back of his throat. "Ruby has been in ICU at Southside Medical Center since yesterday morning."

That got Lincoln's attention. Making sure his hood remained in place, he spun to face the lawyer. His voice came out louder than expected. "Is she all right?"

"Yes," Templeton quickly amended. "It's her brother. He was in an accident."

Lincoln studied the lawyer's face for long moments. "Will he live?"

The lawyer shrugged. "That, I can't answer. What I do know, however, is that the boy has no insurance, and that DCF has been called in."

A strange feeling overcame Lincoln, but he quickly shook it off. "Department of Children and Families? Why are they involved?"

"Ruby doesn't have legal guardianship of the boy. Technically, that makes him a ward of the state."

Lincoln should have gained more satisfaction from the news than he was currently feeling. He blamed it on the lack of sleep he'd gotten since Ruby's visit. "Keep me posted on everything that has to do with her or the boy."

"Understood. Is there anything else I can do, such as speed up the process with DCF?"

Lincoln wasn't sure what made him shake his head. "No. DCF doesn't interest me."

"If I may, sir?"

The Beast watched him closely from beneath his hood. "I'm listening."

Templeton shifted his weight and pushed his glasses up on his nose. "If the child is removed from the home, I believe the sister would do anything in her power to get him back. Anything."

Understanding suddenly dawned. If Ruby lost her brother to the system, she would have to go through the proper legal channels to get him back. And without money, the process could take months, maybe even years. Which would leave her no choice but to accept Lincoln's earlier offer.

But something about removing the injured child from his sister's care left a bad taste in Lincoln's mouth. Though it shouldn't. Were it not for the Atwoods, Lincoln would never had become the beast he was today.

"Leave the boy be. Ruby will come around. Of that, I have no doubt."

"Are you sure about that?"

The Beast stalked forward, stopping mere inches from a startled Templeton. He hovered above him, forcing the lawyer to tilt his head back to see him. "Do not ever question me again. You work for me, Templeton. Do not forget that."

Templeton's Adam's apple bobbed up and down his thin neck. "I-I apologize for overstepping my bounds. It won't happen again."

Lincoln stood there for several more heartbeats and then spun back toward the window. "I will have Ruby Atwood, one way or another. Her humiliation is just the beginning, Templeton. If I am to be a monster for the rest of my life, then she will spend the rest of her days realizing just how much of a monster I truly am."

"Very good, sir. Whatever you require of me, you need only ask. I will serve you as I served your father before you."

Lincoln's eyes slid shut at the mention of his father. He blamed Stanford Barone for his curse as much as he blamed Agatha Atwood. But neither of them still lived. There was no one left to pay the price of his torment but Ruby Atwood. And pay, she would...

* * * *

Another day came and went without any word from Ruby.

The Beast continued to prowl the halls of his dark mansion, agitated and restless.

He couldn't seem to stop thinking about the young, infuriating hazel-eyed beauty.

No matter how much he wanted to wrap his hands around her throat and squeeze the life from her, he knew he couldn't. Not without disgracing her first.

Ruby Atwood's scent was stuck in his brain. He couldn't shake the tantalizing essence of her, the soft, clean fragrance he'd encountered in her room the night he had slipped in unannounced.

Angry that she affected him in such a way, Lincoln stormed from the house and headed straight for the river.

He didn't care who saw him. Nothing else mattered but ridding his mind of the light-haired beauty with the luminous eyes.

With a snarl of disgust, the Beast practically ripped the cloak from his shoulders, yanked off his shirt, and toed off his boots. His jeans took a bit longer to maneuver with the jerky movements of his fingers.

The cool water of the river felt amazing on his overheated skin. He dove beneath the surface, popping up somewhere in the center.

Pushing his hair back away from his face, Lincoln opened his eyes only to find the lights of the French Quarter mocking him from the distance. Ruby was amidst those lights.

"Blast you," he growled, fighting the howl rising in his throat. He hated himself for allowing her to get under his skin. And she seemed to be embedded there as of late.

Chapter Fourteen

"Ruby?" Mrs. Fleming's voice penetrated Ruby's sleep-fogged brain. "Wake up, love."

Stretching her cramped legs out in front of her, Ruby opened her eyes and blinked up at her elderly neighbor. "Hi, Mrs. Fleming. What are you doing here?"

"I came to sit with Cameron so that you could go home and get some sleep."

Ruby shook her head. "I can't leave him. He might—"

"You're going to be lying right beside him if you don't get something to eat and some sleep. Not to mention, you need a shower. I can smell you from here."

Ruby checked her watch. She'd been asleep for almost an hour. "I can't go home yet, Mrs. Fleming. I have to meet with the funeral director about Daddy's burial arrangements. But I would appreciate you sitting with Cameron for a bit while I get that done."

"Of course, dear. I'll stay for as long as you need me."

Pushing to her feet, Ruby stretched her aching muscles and grabbed her wallet. She took one last look at her brother before striding from the room.

She rode the elevator to the first floor, grabbed a cup of coffee, and left the hospital.

Gaskin's Funeral Home was thankfully on Canal Street, about three blocks up from the hospital.

The closer Ruby got to the funeral home, the more nauseated she became.

She took a fortifying breath and stopped in front of the massive oak doors.

You can do this, she told herself, pulling the handle and stepping inside. Her father had been dead for four days now. She was running out of time.

"May I help you?" An older man dressed impeccably in a black suit stepped forward.

Ruby swallowed hard and met the man's patient-looking gaze. "My name is Ruby Atwood. We spoke yesterday about my father's funeral arrangements."

"Ah yes, Miss Atwood. Right this way."

Ruby followed him to a small office off to the right and took a seat behind an immaculate desk with a black nameplate that read *LANCE TRUMAN.*

"I am truly sorry for your loss, Miss Atwood. Losing a loved one is difficult enough without the worries of burial arrangements. That's what I'm here for. Let's start off by getting a feel of what you're looking for."

"The cheapest thing you have," Ruby whispered, unable to hold his gaze. "My father didn't have any burial insurance."

Mr. Truman shifted in his seat and opened a thick catalog that sat in front of him on his desk. "I see. These are the least expensive coffins we carry." He gently pushed the catalog across the desk in front of Ruby.

"Two thousand dollars?" Ruby gasped, finally meeting the funeral director's gaze. "That's the cheapest you have?"

"I'm afraid so, Miss Atwood. Your only other option would be cremation."

Ruby's stomach lurched. "I can't have him cremated, Mr. Truman. We're Catholic. Cremation isn't an option."

"I meant no offense," the funeral director assured her, nodding toward the catalog, "but the cheapest service we can do will cost around six thousand dollars. And that's foregoing a viewing."

"Six thousand dollars?" Ruby choked out in disbelief. "But you just said two thousand."

"The coffin itself is two thousand," Mr. Truman corrected. "The entire funeral will run around six thousand. And that's without tax."

Tears threatened, but Ruby forced them back. She was out of options, and frankly…out of steam.

She stood on unsteady legs. "I'll be in touch."

Rushing from the office, Ruby burst through the wooden doors, staggered off down the sidewalk, and ducked into an alley.

The tears began to fall in earnest. Panic welled up inside her chest, choking her in its intensity.

Ruby couldn't breathe. Great racking sobs consumed her, forcing her to lean against the wall for support.

A wail wrenched from her, and her legs collapsed beneath her. She slid to the ground in a mindless heap of grief and agony.

Unsure of how long she lay there, falling apart in that alley, Ruby pushed to her feet and numbly walked back to the hospital.

She took the elevator back to the third floor.

"Ruby?" Mrs. Fleming began as Ruby stepped into Cameron's room, only to be interrupted by a steely-eyed demon in a floral print skirt.

"Are you the boy's sister?" the newcomer in the room questioned without blinking.

Ruby could only nod, anxiety over the woman's presence seizing her voice.

"My name is Mrs. Goodson. I'm here on behalf of the Department of Children and

Families. Custody of your brother has been temporarily given over to the state of Louisiana."

The room began to spin, leaving Ruby no choice but to grip the back of a chair to remain on her feet. "You can't take him from me."

"Anytime something of this magnitude, involving a child presents itself, we must investigate. After speaking with his teachers, several of your neighbors, and the hospital staff, it's been determined that the child's safety is at risk."

"But it was an accident," Ruby breathed, moving closer to her brother's side. "It could have happened to anyone. Please, give me another chance!"

"I suggest you get your affairs in order, Miss Atwood. You will be notified once a hearing has been set up. It'll be up to a judge whether you're fit to care for your brother."

Moving to the door, Mrs. Goodson turned back to face Ruby. "A piece of advice? Make sure you have a job, a stable home, and sufficient afterschool care for the child if you cannot be there. Those are the terms a judge will require before releasing your brother into your care."

Ruby stood frozen to the spot, unable to move, to even breathe. It took Mrs. Fleming several attempts at calling her name to penetrate Ruby's terrified mind.

Ruby met her worried neighbor's gaze. "What am I going to do?"

Mrs. Fleming shuffled over to Ruby's side and gently took hold of her hand. "Don't worry, sweet girl. Everything will work out. You'll see. First things first, the judge won't require you have a job if you have sufficient funds to care for Cameron. I'm sure your daddy had savings set aside to—"

"We're broke," Ruby interrupted, fighting the dreaded tears once more. "It's all gone. Everything, Mrs. Fleming. Including the house."

The elderly woman's face turned the color of her white blouse. "Gone?"

"Daddy gambled it all away. Every penny, even the house. He also let the insurance lapse. Now I have no way of paying for Cameron's medical bills. The surgery alone was over one hundred thousand dollars. That's not including the X-rays, medications, anesthesiologist, and the extended stay in ICU. Not to mention, Cameron's going to need therapy."

Lincoln Barone's proposal abruptly floated through Ruby's mind. *"One month with me, and I'll give you the house along with all the money your father lost to gambling."*

"Ruby?" Mrs. Fleming was saying, her eyes huge with shock. "What are you going to do?"

"I don't know, Mrs. Fleming. Would you mind sitting with Cam for a few hours? I need to go home and shower. I have a lot to think over."

Mrs. Fleming wrapped Ruby in a tight hug. "Take all the time you need, sweetheart. I won't leave him."

Backing up a step, the elderly neighbor pulled a small wad of cash from her skirt pocket and placed it in Ruby's hand.

Blinking back the ever-present tears, Ruby shook her head. "I can't take your money, Mrs. Fleming."

"Nonsense. You'll need cab fare as well as something to eat. Now go on, you're losing daylight."

Ruby reluctantly stuffed the bills into her wallet and kissed Mrs. Fleming's cheek.

"I don't know how to thank you."

"No thanks needed, my dear."

Ruby ran from the room before she broke down once again.

Chapter Fifteen

Ruby emerged from the shower, applied a small amount of makeup, pulled on a pink sundress, and slipped on a pair of white sandals.

The dark circles beneath her eyes weren't as noticeable under the foundation.

After brushing her teeth, she smeared on some lip gloss and snatched up her wallet along with her cell. She would go talk to Spencer.

If anyone could help her figure out a way out of the mess she was now in, it would be Spencer Wright. Hopefully, his father would let her work some hours in his gift shop.

Locking up the house, Ruby walked the short distance over to Royal Street and knocked on Spencer's door.

When no answer came, she knocked again and then tried the knob. The door opened with ease.

"Hello?" Ruby softly called, stepping into the foyer.

Muffled voices sounded from upstairs, followed by a barely audible feminine giggle.

"Spencer?"

More laughter ensued.

Ruby quietly moved up the stairs, drawn to the high-pitched squeals that floated down to meet her.

She stopped outside Spencer's bedroom door, hesitantly turned the knob, and eased the door open an inch.

Her mind instantly rebelled against the scene that unfolded before her.

Spencer Wright lay beneath the covers, smiling at a beautiful brunette, lying beside him.

A hoarse cry escaped Ruby, calling attention from the occupants on the bed.

"Ruby," Spencer breathed, frozen in obvious shock.

He threw the covers back and scrambled unceremoniously from the bed. "Ruby, wait!"

Ruby spun on her heel and fled. She ran down the stairs, jerked the front door open, and darted down the sidewalk, all the while closing off her mind to Spencer's persistent pleading.

After several blocks of blindly running, Ruby found herself at the banks of the river. Darkness had fallen, giving way to the rising moon.

She stared into the inky black waves of the water, her eyes dry as sand. There were no more tears left to cry.

Her cell phone abruptly rang, shattering the remaining grip she had on reality.

A scream ricocheted through the night, a horrifying sound that seemed to go on forever. Ruby numbly realized it came from her.

She staggered back a few feet, shivering, though the night air remained warm on her skin.

"Hey, lady? Are you all right?"

Somewhere in the depths of Ruby's mind, she knew a man spoke to her, but she couldn't bring herself to acknowledge him.

Her limbs stayed frozen to the spot, her gaze locked on the ever-moving river. Or was it sealed to the mansion on the other side?

Summoning what little inner strength she had left, Ruby waved off the concerned bystander and stumbled along the riverbank to the ferry up ahead.

She dug some bills that Mrs. Fleming had given her, from her wallet and paid the fee before stepping on board.

Ruby barely remembered the ride across the river, her mind replaying the last week's events in torturous detail.

She suddenly found herself standing on the doorstep of Lincoln Barone, her knuckles rapping on the wood.

The door quickly opened, and the housekeeper Ruby had met days before answered the door. "Miss Atwood?"

Ruby stared at her in a daze, her voice sounding wooden to her own ears. "I'm here to see Mr. Barone."

Glancing behind her, the housekeeper remained in the door as if blocking Ruby's view. "The master's busy at the moment."

"The master?" Ruby repeated in a stupor.

"Mrs. Tuff," a cloak-covered Barone rasped, stepping up behind the housekeeper and pulling the door wide. "Go see about dinner."

Ruby peered into the darkened depths of his hood, yet nothing could be seen but shadows.

Barone stood completely still.

"I accept," Ruby whispered, lifting her chin. "I accept your proposal."

Lincoln stepped back and jerked his chin toward the stairs. "Go to my study."

A shudder passed through Ruby that had nothing to do with the night air. Something about the cloaked figure of Lincoln Barone intimidated her to her bones.

She brushed past him and strode stiffly to the stairs, the sound of the door closing behind her sealing her fate.

Ruby knew she'd never be the same after that night, that her life would forever be changed. But Lincoln Barone had the power to help her brother, and Ruby would do anything to obtain it.

Taking a fortifying breath, she marched up the stairs and took a right into the same room Barone had proposed his offer to her before.

He was suddenly there, close behind her, stopping with his chest against her back.

Ruby could feel the heat of his skin seeping through his cloak to penetrate her thin sundress.

His hands came up to rest on her upper arms. "Are you certain you can do this, Ruby Atwood? Because once you agree to my terms, there will be no turning back."

Her stomach flipped at his words. She stared straight ahead at the dark design of a painting on the opposite wall. Images of Cameron lying in that hospital bed flashed through her mind.

No matter what happened to her, what she had to endure at the hands of Lincoln Barone, Ruby refused to lose her brother.

She swallowed back her fear. "I'm sure."

Chapter Sixteen

Lincoln's eyes slid shut the moment Ruby murmured those two words. *"I'm sure."*

She was his. There would be no turning back.

He lowered his nose to the top of her head and breathed in her intoxicating scent, his palms coasting down her arms to her hands.

Her trembling wasn't lost on him any more than her stiff posture. "You can relax, Ruby. I'm not going to force you."

"Then what are you going to do to me?"

He smiled beneath the hood. No matter how frightened she truly was of him, she didn't cower away. No, Ruby Atwood had to be the bravest soul Lincoln had ever encountered. Breaking her would prove to be most satisfying.

"Have a seat."

Ruby didn't hesitate. She pulled free of his hold and sat in the chair in front of his desk.

Lincoln casually skirted the big cherrywood desk and took a seat in his own comfortable chair.

Tugging open the bottom drawer, he pulled a folder free and laid it on the desktop.

Ruby watched him without speaking, her intelligent eyes luminous in the lamplight.

Lincoln casually opened the folder and slid it across the desk toward Ruby. "Read over it carefully, and then sign at the bottom."

"What is it?" The slight tremor in her voice, the only evidence of her nervousness.

"It's a contract, giving you everything we discussed upon your last visit. And what I expect from you in return."

He waited while she read over the paper in front of her.

She abruptly leaned back in her seat and stared at him without blinking. "I need your help with my brother. If you can add that in there, you have a deal."

Lincoln's teeth clamped together in irritation. How dare she come into his home with demands. *He* held all the cards in this game.

It took him a second to unclench his teeth enough to speak. "And what would that be?"

"DCF will be placing Cameron in foster care once he's released from the hospital, if I can't prove to be a fit guardian. My brother is the only reason I'm here, Mr. Barone. Not the house, and not the money. Only Cameron."

The Beast wanted to snarl, snatch the little upstart from her seat, and roar in her face that she was there because he allowed it. Certainly not by her own design.

But something held him back. He needed to play his cards right until he had her signature on that contract. "What is it that you would have me do?"

"I want temporary custody of Cameron until the money and house are back in my possession."

"Done."

"Done?" she gasped, her eyebrows going up. "Just like that?"

Lincoln nodded his hood-covered head. "I'll have Templeton take care of it in the morning. Your brother will be moved here for the remainder of his hospital stay. I'll have a doctor and around-the-clock nurses here to see to his needs."

Ruby's mouth fell open. "You can do that?"

"With enough money, one can do anything, Miss Atwood."

Something flickered in her eyes, whether disdain or resentment, he couldn't be sure. "What's the catch?"

"You will move in as well."

"Of course. I wouldn't dream of leaving Cameron alone. I—"

"In my room," Lincoln interrupted, cutting off the rest of her words.

She visibly swallowed. "I had assumed as much."

"Then we are on the same page. You need only to sign the bottom line."

Lincoln narrowed his gaze beneath the hood, watching as Ruby picked up a pen.

Her hand hovered over the signature line for a heartbeat before she raised her gaze to him once more. "I want to see your face."

The Beast recoiled from her words. "No."

"No?"

Lincoln surged to his feet, careful to keep his hood in place. "I own you, Miss Atwood, not the other way around. Either sign the document or get out!"

Ruby flinched but didn't run. With resolve in her incredible eyes, she scrawled her name on the dotted line and laid the pen aside. "Now, what?"

The Beast was momentarily speechless. He'd waited a lifetime for this moment, yet somehow, he thought it would feel more satisfying. "Come with me."

Without waiting for Ruby to stand, Lincoln exited his office and entered his massive bedroom.

The sound of Ruby's footsteps clicking on the hardwood floors behind him assured him that she'd followed.

He nodded toward a large armoire against the far wall. "Everything you will need for your stay is in there. Dinner will be served in twenty minutes. I expect you to be changed and ready to eat by the time I return."

Turning toward the door, he brushed past her, stopping just inside the hallway. "You will wear the silver dress. I'll send Mrs. Tuff in to help you."

The Beast took the stairs to the kitchen where Mrs. Tuff stood stirring something in a yellow bowl. "Miss Atwood needs your assistance."

"Goodness, you frightened me," Mrs. Tuff gasped, dropping the spoon she held with a clatter against the side of the bowl. "Will Miss Atwood be staying for dinner?"

Lincoln didn't hesitate. "She will be here for quite some time. Do not ask questions, and do not interfere. No matter what. Do I make myself clear?"

Mrs. Tuff lowered her gaze and gave a swift nod. "Yes, sir."

"Now, go help Ruby dress for dinner. She's to wear the silver dress, the silver slippers, and the undergarments on the far-left side of the top drawer."

The housekeeper stiffened but didn't argue. "Right away, Mr. Barone."

"And Mrs. Tuff?" Lincoln called out as she reached the archway leading into the den.

"Yes?"

"Miss Atwood has been paid very well for her services. Remember that before you think to pity her."

The housekeeper swiftly nodded and rushed from the room.

Chapter Seventeen

Ruby hadn't moved since Lincoln Barone had left the room a few minutes before. Her gaze touched on everything from the red velvet canopy hanging above the biggest bed Ruby had ever seen, to the glass-covered, dead rose sitting on a small table near the window.

"Miss Atwood." The housekeeper sailed into the room in a flurry of skirts.

Or was that an apron over her skirt? Ruby wondered with a quick glance. "Yes."

"We weren't properly introduced before. My name is Mrs. Tuff. I'm the housekeeper of this ginormous house. I also do the cooking for Mr. Barone."

Ruby attempted a smile but failed.

"Well, no matter," the housekeeper continued as if the awkward moment hadn't just happened. "The master has sent me to help you get ready for dinner."

Ruby glanced at the armoire. "What's wrong with what I have on?"

"There's nothing wrong with it, my dear. But the master wants you to wear the silver dress, and — "

"The master?" Ruby blurted, effectively cutting her off. "That's the third time I've heard you refer to him as such."

Mrs. Tuff ignored her, moving instead to the armoire and tugging on the doors.

Ruby's mouth dropped open in awe. At least twenty obviously expensive, utterly incredible dresses hung before her.

Clearing her throat to hide her shock, Ruby studied the rest of the contents in silence.

Shoes of every style and color lined the bottom of the antique wardrobe, along with an array of other clothes neatly folded on the top shelf.

Apparently old man Barone had known she would come crawling to him long before she did.

Bitterness nearly choked her. It took every ounce of courage she had to remain in that room, when all she wanted was to run from that place and never look back.

But she couldn't. Cameron needed her, and he was all that mattered in that moment.

Mrs. Tuff extracted the beautiful, silver dress from the armoire and laid it on the massive bed. She then opened a drawer and withdrew some other items of clothing before sliding out a narrower drawer and plucking some jewels from their velvety homes.

After snagging a pair of silver high-heeled sandals from the bottom, she turned to face

Ruby. "Would you like some help getting out of your dress?"

Ruby shook her head. "I can do it myself. There's no need for you to stay."

Mrs. Tuff's gaze nervously shifted toward the door. "Mr. Barone ordered me to help you."

"I see," Ruby muttered sarcastically. "We wouldn't want to disappoint his majesty."

The housekeeper's expression would have been comical at any other time. Not tonight.

Giving Mrs. Tuff her back, Ruby untied the shoulder strings to her sundress and stepped out of it.

A blush stained her cheeks as she stood before the woman in nothing but a pair of cotton, white panties and her sandals.

"You will wear this. It goes beneath the dress."

Covering herself as best she could, Ruby half turned toward the bed to take in the garment displayed there.

It appeared to be some sort of white bustier with a small silver bow between the bra cups.

Swallowing hard, Ruby lifted her gaze to the blushing housekeeper. "Is this really necessary?"

"I think it only appropriate since you don't have a bra."

Ruby turned away, unable to face the housekeeper another second. She reached behind her with trembling fingers. "Give it to me, please."

Mrs. Tuff thankfully didn't speak as Ruby, toed off her shoes and donned the bustier. She pulled on a pair of hose next and held out her hand once more. "The dress."

"It's not too late to run," Mrs. Tuff whispered in her ear, slipping the shimmery material over Ruby's head. "Run and never look back."

Ruby turned her head and met the housekeeper's gaze. "I can't. The stakes are far too high for me to run now."

Compassion shone from Mrs. Tuff's brown eyes. "Find another way, girl. There's always another way."

"Not for me, there isn't."

Ruby allowed Mrs. Tuff to finish helping her dress. Everything fit her to a T. Even the shoes were a perfect fit.

"Sit right here," the housekeeper gently demanded, patting the cushion of a bench perched in front a mirrorless vanity.

"What happened to the mirror?"

Mrs. Tuff looked away, but not before Ruby saw the anxiety on her face.

The housekeeper returned and slipped something around Ruby's neck.

"Are these real?" Ruby gasped, lifting the sparkling diamond necklace up to the light.

"They were the master's mothers. Hold still."

Ruby held completely still, allowing the housekeeper to drape a shiny, silver chain with a stunning diamond dangling from it, over her head. She could feel the cool, heavy gem resting against her forehead.

"There. All done."

Had it not been for the circumstances surrounding her, Ruby would have otherwise enjoyed her attire.

She stood and followed Mrs. Tuff to the stairs.

A cloaked Lincoln waited at the bottom of the stairs, still as death, with only a whisper-soft intake of breath. Evidence that he approved of Ruby's attire.

Ruby stopped in front of him, waiting for him to tell her what to do next.

He remained unmoving.

She glanced back at Mrs. Tuff, hoping the housekeeper would give her a clue as to what he expected her to do, when he finally spoke.

But his words weren't directed at her. "Once dinner has been served, I want you to take the night off, Mrs. Tuff. I don't wish to be disturbed for any reason. Be sure to let the others know as well."

Ruby's heart jumped into her throat. He wanted everyone out of the house but her. Did that mean he planned on hurting her? Torturing her?

"You need not fear, Ruby Atwood," Barone rumbled, apparently reading her thoughts. "I have no intensions of harming you."

Ruby prayed he spoke the truth. Though she knew him to be older, the body beneath that cloak was huge. At least six-feet-six with shoulders to rival a linebacker's. Yeah, he could snap her like a twig if he took a notion to.

Chapter Eighteen

The Beast waited for Mrs. Tuff to traipse off into the kitchen before lifting a glove-covered hand toward Ruby.

He was still finding it hard to breathe after the vision of her appearing at the top of those stairs.

She accepted his gesture of assistance, but the rebellious light he'd come to know still shone bright in her eyes.

Lincoln found that he liked her rebellious spirit. It would make breaking her that much more thrilling.

"You're a vision, Miss Atwood."

"I can't say the same, Grim."

Lincoln's lips twitched beneath his cloak. Oh, how he was going to enjoy bending her to his will.

Instead of seating Ruby at one end of the table as was customary, Lincoln escorted her to the chair next to his.

Helping her sit, he took his own seat at the head of the overly large table and offered her some wine.

Ruby shook her head. "No, thank you."

Tightening his jaw in resolve, Lincoln plucked up her glass and poured her a healthy amount of the sweet red wine. "I insist."

"Are you always this bossy?"

Her question angered him. "You are here at my bidding. You will do as you're told without question. If you can't follow that one simple rule, you are welcome to leave right now."

Ruby lifted her chin and picked up her glass. She peered at him over the rim while draining its contents.

Lincoln knew she drank the wine out of spite.

It mattered not.

Mrs. Tuff bustled into the room with Stiles tight on her heels. They set several dishes in the center of the table and then bid their master a good night.

Lincoln waved them off without a glance, his gaze glued to the beauty at his side.

It took everything he had not to wrap his hand in her hair and kiss her angry mouth.

Lincoln looked away lest he embarrass himself and do just that.

Dinner consisted of roasted duck and new potatoes cooked in a light sherry sauce. There were green peas, homemade bread, and banana pudding for dessert.

"Eat," he demanded, nodding toward the food in the center of the table.

Ruby flinched, but kept her stubborn chin held high.

To Lincoln's surprise, she uncovered the duck and helped herself to a nice-sized portion. She then added potatoes, some peas, and a chunk of bread.

Refilling her wineglass, the Beast piled his own plate high with food and ate without further delay.

He watched Ruby from beneath the hood of his cloak, eat like a woman starved. He wondered how long it had been since she'd last eaten. Or perhaps she ate out of relief that her brother would soon be back in her arms.

Lincoln studied her movements, the confidence with which she carried herself. She had an inner strength that showed in the set of her jaw, the flash of her eyes.

Once the meal had been finished, Lincoln refilled Ruby's wineglass, plucked it from the table, and stood.

The stiff set to her shoulders wasn't lost on him.

"Come."

Ruby slowly pushed back from the table and got to her feet without looking at him.

With her back straight, she moved to the stairs, the fingers holding on to the banister slightly trembling.

Lincoln followed her up. "Have a seat on the bed."

Taking an unsteady breath, Ruby moved to the side of the bed and sat, looking for all the world like she could bolt at any second.

The Beast lowered to his knees in front of her, lifted each of her tiny feet in his hands, and removed her shoes.

She seemed surprised by the gesture, but she didn't speak.

Rising to his full height, he pulled his own boots off and carefully lowered his great weight onto the bed near the headboard. He took hold of Ruby's hand. "Look at me."

"Why won't you show me your face?" she blurted.

Lincoln ground his teeth. "It's better this way."

"Better for whom?"

Unable to respond, he continued to watch her from the safety of the hood. She looked terrified and lost.

Lincoln had never craved anything as bad as he craved Ruby Atwood. He wanted nothing more than to keep her there for as long as he possibly could.

"What now?" she whispered so softly he almost didn't hear.

"There's a nightgown in the armoire. Put it on."

Lincoln waited patiently while she retrieved the gown, slipped into the bathroom and changed into it.

She returned to the room without looking at him and draped the shimmery, silver dress over the back of a chair.

Sliding over to give her room, the Beast pulled back the covers, crawled beneath, and held them open. "Get in bed."

Ruby's shoulders sagged in defeat. She turned toward the bed and lifted her knee to the mattress.

Was that a tear in her eye?

An odd sense of shame washed over him, triggering his anger.

"Get up here," he snapped, jerking the covers back even more.

Ruby jumped, scrambling into the bed so fast she bumped his chin with her head.

Lying flat on her back, she stared up at the ceiling without moving. "Can you please make it quick?"

Lincoln blinked, not liking this side of her at all. He preferred her snark, her ire, her anger...anything but the fear and despondency now lining her voice.

Pushing her to her side, he brought his arms around her and jerked her back against him in a spooning position.

She stiffened but didn't attempt to pull away.

Why had he allowed her desperation to get to him? He'd waited his whole life to exact his revenge on an Atwood, and now that he had one in his grasp, he couldn't seem to humiliate her as he'd planned.

Shock seeped into his pores as the realization of his feelings unfolded. He didn't want Ruby against her will... He wanted her to want him, to feel for him what he was beginning to feel for her.

But that would never happen if she ever got a look at him. Of that, the Beast was certain.

Chapter Nineteen

Ruby blinked into the darkness, still reeling from what had just happened. Or rather, what hadn't happened.

What was Barone doing? Spooning her? She wanted more than anything to ask him what his plans for her were, yet she was too afraid of angering him.

She held completely still, dozens of questions running through her mind. Had he gone to sleep?

Ruby wasn't sure how long she lay there before her eyes grew heavy and sleep finally claimed her...

* * * *

Warm. Ruby was uncomfortably warm. She moved away from the heat, only to have it follow her.

A soft touch on her arm wrenched a moan from her throat. She sighed in her sleep and rolled to her back.

The touch continued, drawing lazy circles on her shoulder.

A restlessness set in, coaxing her to turn more toward the warmth.

"Ruby..."

The raspy growl of her name tickled at the edges of her semiconscious state.

The caress deepened, as did the voice hovering above her. "You smell so good."

Ruby's eyes flew open to stare up at the hooded face of Lincoln Barone.

"What are you doing?" She recoiled from his touch.

"Nothing that you didn't like," he growled, his voice raspy from sleep.

Afraid to move, Ruby watched him in leery silence, praying he wouldn't force her to finish what she'd apparently started.

Lincoln pulled away, keeping his cloaked upper body hidden in the shadows of the bed's canopy. "Get up."

Those were all the words Ruby needed to hear.

She jumped from the bed, nearly falling in her haste.

"Take what clothes you will need from the armoire and shower if you want."

With a quick nod, Ruby moved to the armoire, grabbed a pair of shorts, a red T-shirt, and some running shoes. Plucking out a pair of socks, she rummaged through, searching for some undergarments.

"What is it?" Lincoln rasped from behind the half-open canopy.

A blush spread up Ruby's face. "There are no undergarments in here."

"I'll send Mrs. Tuff to town to pick up whatever you need. In the meantime, you will just have to make do."

She hurried off toward the bathroom before he changed his mind and hauled her back to finish what had almost happened in her sleep.

Safely behind the bathroom door, Ruby engaged the lock, slipped out of the gown and turned on the shower.

The hot spray of the water felt good on her skin. She'd made it through the night without being mauled by Lincoln Barone.

Ruby tilted her head back under the powerful spray and closed her eyes.

The warm sluice of water traveling down her body reminded her of Lincoln's touch on her upper arm.

Had he not spoken her name, she would have unknowingly allowed him to continue touching her. *Had* it been unknowingly? Had her subconscious somehow known?

Her eyes flew open, and she jerked her head from the spray. What was happening to her? The stress from everything that she'd experienced over the past week had obviously addled her mind.

Snatching up the shampoo, Ruby quickly washed her hair and then used the liquid soap to cleanse her body.

She tried to push what had happened in that bed from her mind, but the harder she tried, the more she dwelled on it.

Goose bumps spread across her skin, and heat traveled up her neck into her face.

The sound of the knob jiggling could be heard over the spray of the shower. She quickly finished rinsing, pulled back the curtain, and stepped over the side of the old claw-foot tub. "I'll be right out."

"Don't ever lock me out again."

Blast him, Ruby silently cursed, drying off and wrapping her hair in the towel. She pulled on the white shorts and red T-shirt and then sat on the toilet lid to don her shoes.

The door suddenly opened, and Barone stepped into the room, holding a key in his hand. He reached over without warning and plucked the towel from her head. "Stand up."

Ruby hesitated.

"Stand!"

She jumped to her feet. "What are you going to do?"

"I told you, no questions. As long as you do exactly as I say, you won't be harmed." He turned to go. "Come."

Following a short distance behind, Ruby nearly ran into him when he abruptly stopped in front of the bench she'd sat on the night before.

"Sit."

Ruby took a seat on the bench and stared into the mirrorless vanity in front of her.

Barone gently ran a brush through her hair, sending her mouth to drop open in shock.

Confused by the gesture, Ruby attempted to make small talk. "Why is there no mirror in the vanity?"

He ignored her, all the while continuing to carefully brush her hair.

"So, we're going to spend the next month together without talking?"

The brushing momentarily stopped before beginning once more. "I don't like mirrors."

She thought about that for a second. "Are you scarred or something?"

"Something," he murmured, tilting her head back to get to her bangs.

Ruby frowned at the ceiling. Had he been burned or in an accident that disfigured him? She'd seen his pictures on the wall. He had no scars to speak of in any of them. "I didn't see any scars in your photos."

He paused once again. "My photos?"

"On the stairwell wall."

"The portraits you saw were of my father, Stanford Barone."

Ruby's stomach tightened in anxiety. If the pictures on the wall belong to his father, then Lincoln couldn't be much older than her. "How old are you?"

"I will be thirty in less than a month."

He was still ten years her senior, but nothing even close to what she'd originally thought.

If he was that young, why had he not followed through with his threat of making her his? Not that she was complaining. It simply made no sense.

"Once we have had breakfast, I will call Templeton and have him take care of your brother's medical bills. As soon as he is released from ICU, he will be moved here."

Ruby's heart lurched. "How are you going to pull that off?"

"You let me worry about that. Go downstairs and eat your breakfast. I'm going to shower."

Ruby watched him walk past her and disappear into the bathroom.

What a strange man, she thought, gaining her feet. One minute he was the world's biggest creep, and the next, he was brushing her hair.

Chapter Twenty

Lincoln entered the dining room in time to watch Ruby finish off the last bite of her pancakes.

She stiffened the moment she noticed him, but didn't look up from her empty plate.

He pulled his hood lower over his face. "Arrangements have been set in motion for your brother."

Ruby lifted her head. "I need to go to the hospital today. He'll be terrified if he wakes and I'm not there."

"He is already awake," Lincoln informed her, taking a seat at the head of the table. "And you are not leaving."

Desperation flashed in her eyes. "He's just a kid, Mr. Barone. He needs me."

I need you too, Lincoln wanted to shout back, but instead he said, "You stay here."

For some reason, the disappointment evident on her face didn't please him as it should have. "I'll have Templeton put a rush on it."

Why was he bending to her every demand? Lincoln wondered in no small amount of agitation. She was an Atwood, a descendant of Agatha, and the spawn of Charles.

"But that could take days. Please, Mr. Barone, let me see my brother?"

Lincoln slammed his fist down onto the tabletop. "I said no!"

Ruby surged to her feet and ran from the room, the sound of her footsteps echoing throughout the walls of the overly large house.

She ran upstairs, slamming his bedroom door behind her.

His bedroom, he silently acknowledged, leaving the table as well.

Lincoln stormed up the stairs, gripped the knob to his bedroom door, and jerked it open. He would set her straight once and for all.

He opened his mouth, intending on scaring her into submission, when his gaze landed on her small body huddled in the center of his bed.

The sounds of her crying reached him before he crossed over the threshold.

He took a hesitant step forward, and then another. "Ruby?"

"Leave me alone." She sniffed, lying on her side with her back to him.

Lincoln flinched as if slapped, angry that he'd allowed her words to affect him. "Fine. You can lie up here and cry the rest of the day. It won't change anything."

"How can you be so cruel?" Ruby sat up to face him, the tears swimming in her eyes a testament to her pain.

"Cruel?" the Beast snarled. "You want to speak of cruelty to me? Where were the tears for the innocent baby born into a curse? A baby so huge that even his own mother died giving birth to him. A child so ugly, he couldn't attend school with the other children. Where were the tears then, Ruby!"

Lincoln staggered back, stunned that he'd revealed so much to her.

Ruby moved closer to the edge of the bed, her face growing paler by the second. "Were you that baby?"

Unable to bear her pity, Lincoln stormed from the room and stumbled into his study, slamming the door closed behind him.

He jerked up a glass and poured himself a shot of bourbon. What had gotten into him? He'd spilled his guts to the one person he couldn't handle pity from. Why had he lost control in such a way?

A timid knock sounded, yanking the Beast out of his self-loathing party. "Go away."

Stunned to see the door crack open, Lincoln downed his drink and stormed around his desk. "I said go away!"

Ruby's pale, drawn face appeared through the opening.

Lincoln spun toward the window, giving her his back. "What do you want?"

"I want to see my brother."

Another growl rumbled in his chest. "You are not to leave this house."

The creaking of the floor let him know she'd entered his study. "What happened to you to make you so cruel?"

The Beast's shoulder's stiffened. "Leave it alone, Ruby."

She stopped directly behind him. "I want to know."

He slowly turned to face her, rage simmering in his gut. "I am the thing of nightmares, a beast, cursed before birth to walk this earth in shadows. A curse placed upon me by your grandmother, Agatha Atwood."

Ruby's already pale face turned a shade whiter if that were possible. "What are you talking about? What curse?"

"This!" he roared, snatching the hood back from his face.

Ruby gasped, staggering back a step. Her eyes were huge and horror filled.

She took another step back, her hand blindly reaching behind her. She bumped into the chair in front of the desk, nearly falling in her haste to skirt around it.

"Is this what you wanted so badly to see?" he snarled, stalking her toward the door. "Well, now you've seen it, and now you know why you're here!"

Shaking her head in denial, Ruby stopped at the door. "It's not possible."

"Get out."

"I can't," Ruby whispered, more tears filling her eyes.

The Beast closed the gap between them, leaned down until his nose nearly touched hers, and roared in her face. "Get out, and don't ever come back!"

With a cry of terror, Ruby turned and ran. She hit the stairs wide open and didn't stop until the front door shut behind her.

Lincoln stood where he was, his breath punching in and out of his chest. He'd lost control, done the unthinkable and scared Ruby away.

"What have I done?"

Chapter Twenty-One

Ruby ran from the Barone mansion as fast as her legs would carry her. She bypassed the ferry for the bridge. She had no money on her, and her cell phone was in Lincoln's bedroom along with her wallet.

But there was no way she was going back after them.

Visions of Lincoln's monstrous face flashed through her mind again and again. He'd accused her grandmother of being responsible.

He's insane, Ruby realized, running along the bike path of the bridge that would take her home. There was no such thing as curses. Especially ones that took the humanity in a person and left a beast in its place.

And Ruby knew him to be a beast. He wasn't some deformed man with a few disfigured facial features. He reminded her of a werewolf she'd watched in a movie as a child.

Except for his eyes. He had the most beautiful eyes she'd ever seen. Big electric blue eyes fringed in long, dark lashes.

She slowed her step. Ruby had seen pain in those giant blue eyes.

Glancing behind her, Ruby realized she'd run at least two miles. She came to a stop, rested her hands on her knees, and attempted to catch her breath.

A truck pulled over next to her and rolled down the passenger side window. "Do you need a ride?"

Ruby squinted against the bright light of the sun and studied the man's face. He looked to be in his early sixties. "I'm going to Royal Street."

"Hop in," he offered, opening the door for her. "That's not far."

Ruby climbed into the air-conditioned cab of the man's truck and closed the door. "Thank you so much. It was getting pretty warm out there."

"It sure is. Did your car break down somewhere? You look like you've been walking for miles."

Shaking her head, Ruby sent him a small smile. "I was actually running. Really dumb, I know. Especially on a hot day like today."

The man's gaze softened. He reached up and turned up the air conditioning. "Let's get you cooled off. We'll be on Royal Street shortly."

"Thank you. I really do appreciate this."

Ten minutes later, the truck rolled to a stop in front of Ruby's house. The driver touched her on the arm, concern swimming in his soft brown eyes. "A word of advice from the grandfather of a girl about your age?"

At Ruby's nod, he continued, "Don't ever accept rides from strangers, man or woman."

"I'll remember that," Ruby assured him, thanking him one last time.

After the truck rolled away, Ruby jogged next door to Mrs. Fleming's since she had no key to get into her own house.

"Ruby." Mrs. Fleming opened the door to allow her inside. "Where have you been? I've been worried sick."

"It's a long story, Mrs. Fleming. One that'll have to wait for another time."

The elderly neighbor frowned. "I think you need to make time, else you're going to put me in an early grave."

Ruby sighed and ushered Mrs. Fleming into the kitchen. "Okay, but then I need to hurry to the hospital and check on Cameron."

The next twenty minutes consisted of Ruby drinking iced tea and filling Mrs. Fleming in on everything that had happened over the last twenty-four hours. She left out the part about signing a contract with Lincoln Barone in exchange for helping her and her brother.

"Lincoln Barone, you say?" Mrs. Fleming had paled significantly. "Stanford Barone's child?"

Ruby set her glass of tea on the bar and studied her neighbor's face. "Yes. Do you know him?"

Mrs. Fleming climbed down from her stool and moved to open the refrigerator. "No, but I knew his father. As did your grandmother."

An odd feeling settled in Ruby's gut, Lincoln's words echoing inside her heart. "*I am the thing of nightmares, a beast, cursed before birth to walk this earth in shadows. A curse placed upon me by your grandmother, Agatha Atwood.*"

"What are you not telling me, Ruby?"

"Nothing, Mrs. Fleming. Just some rumor I heard recently. What can you tell me about my grandmother and Stanford Barone?"

Mrs. Fleming shrugged a bony shoulder. "Not a lot. I know there was some bad blood between them."

Ruby picked up her tea and pretended to be interested in the ice swirling in the glass. "Bad blood?"

"It's really not my place to say, Ruby. It's not right for me to speak behind Agatha's back."

Taking a deep breath for patience, Ruby looked up from her tea swirling and met her neighbor's uncomfortable gaze. "Grandmother is dead, Mrs. Fleming. As is my dad. There's no one left to be concerned about."

Mrs. Fleming returned to her seat on the barstool and laid her hand over the top of Ruby's. "Your father was a twin…"

Ten minutes later, Ruby slid from her barstool and rounded the bar. "Thank you for being honest with me. I'd already heard the short version of that story, but I had no idea about Aunt Charlotte or that she even existed, for that matter."

"Yes, well, your grandmother never mentioned her again after she disappeared, and your father was forbidden to speak her name. But Stanford Barone was behind Charlotte's disappearance. Of that, I have no doubt."

"So, the curse against Stanford's unborn child is true then?" Ruby asked in a small voice, needing conformation again.

Mr. Fleming shrugged. "If you believe in that sort of thing. Which, your grandmother did. Voodoo was in Agatha's blood, Ruby. But she began dabbling in other things after her husband passed away."

"Such as?" Ruby prompted, hanging on the elder woman's every word.

"Black magic, for one."

A knock sounded on the door, nearly scaring Ruby out of her skin.

She followed Mrs. Fleming to the foyer as the feeble woman checked the peephole. "Oh, it's Spencer Wright."

Mrs. Fleming opened the door before Ruby could protest.

"Ruby," Spencer breathed, looking over the top of Mrs. Fleming's head. "I've been searching everywhere for you."

Thanking Mrs. Fleming for the tea, Ruby stepped around her and darted out onto the porch. "I have nothing to say to you, Spencer. Now, if you'll excuse me, I need to get to the hospital and see Cam."

"He's not there," Spencer informed her, rushing to catch up with her after she bolted across the street.

Ruby put the brakes on. "What do you mean, he's not there?"

Spencer caught up with her in a few quick steps. "I just left there looking for you. The hospital staff told me that he's been moved to a private location."

The Barone mansion, Ruby guessed, unsure of what to do next. She glanced back at Mrs. Fleming's house and turned to step back into the street.

A sleek black car pulled up beside her with dark, tinted windows. The passenger side window eased down. "Ruby Atwood?"

"Yes?" Ruby answered, leaning down to see inside.

"Get in."

Spencer grabbed on to Ruby's arm as she went to open the back door. "What are you doing?"

She yanked free of his hold. "What needs to be done."

Chapter Twenty-Two

The Beast paced the halls of his mansion while the nurses and staff worked furiously to settle Ruby's brother into a downstairs room.

Templeton had managed to have the boy moved faster than Lincoln would have thought possible, citing, *"Anything can be done with enough money."*

Lincoln hated that Charles Atwood's spawn was now resting under his roof, but he would hate it even more if Ruby never came back.

Curse her for running off the way she had. Not that Lincoln could blame her. He supposed he would have done the same in her shoes. Especially after he'd shown her his beastly face.

"He is all settled in," Templeton informed Lincoln, slipping up behind him.

Lincoln turned to face his attorney. "Any news of Ruby?"

Templeton nodded. "I sent a car to retrieve her. She will be here shortly."

Relieved that she would be returning, Lincoln felt his shoulders slightly relax. "Thank you."

"Of course. Will there be anything else?"

Lincoln thought about that for a second. "I now have temporary custody of the brother?"

"In a manner of speaking," Templeton returned. "I managed to obtain you temporary guardianship over the boy until the sister can acquire custody. If she cannot prove to be a fit guardian, the boy will be a ward of the state."

The Beast absently nodded. "Thank you, Templeton. Once again, you have proven yourself invaluable to me."

"Just doing my job, sir." He turned and left by way of the front door.

Lincoln stood there for long moments after the attorney's departure. Cameron Atwood was now Lincoln's responsibility.

Moving silently through the halls, Lincoln stopped outside Cameron's temporary quarters. He watched through the door as two nurses bustled about while the doctor Lincoln hired stood over the child, checking his vitals.

The sound of the front door crashing open echoed off the walls of the mansion, signaling Ruby's arrival.

"Hello?" she called, the thumping of her heels growing louder by the second. "Mr. Barone?"

"Ruby." Mrs. Tuff intervened. "The master is expecting you."

"Where is he?"

There was a brief hesitation. "Down the hall and to the left."

Lincoln blocked the entrance to Cameron's door when Ruby came rushing around the corner.

"Is Cameron here?"

Waving a hand toward the bedroom he stood in front of, Lincoln answered in a low tone. "The boy is sleeping. You may go in as soon as the doctor is finished checking him over."

Concern flashed in her eyes. "Is he all right?"

"He is going to be fine. I had him sedated for the transfer."

Ruby sagged against the wall behind her. Her eyes briefly slid shut before opening and pinning Lincoln with a grateful gaze. "Not to sound ungrateful after what you just did for Cam, but I would like the terms of the contract amended."

Fury sliced through him. How dare she come storming into his home, making demands after running off as she did. He opened his mouth to tell her as much, but something held him back.

Tilting his cloak-covered head to the side, he fought hard to keep the anger from his voice. "Amended? How so?"

She pushed away from the wall and hesitantly approached him. "I want custody of my brother."

"That is not up to me, Ruby. The judge will make that decision."

"Bull. You add it into the contract that you will do everything in your power to help me obtain sole custody of my brother once the month is up, and I promise you that I will not argue or resist you for the remainder of my stay here."

Though Lincoln wanted nothing more than to laugh at her attempt to bargain with him, he refrained. "Visit with your brother, and then meet me at the boathouse in an hour."

"Does that mean that you'll do it?"

Lincoln moved to step around her. "I'll think about it."

* * * *

Lincoln watched Ruby trail down the slight incline to the boathouse. Although she wore the same clothes she'd had on when she ran off that morning, the color was back in her face, and her light-blonde hair was twisted up into some kind of bun on the back of her head.

"Did you see your brother?" Lincoln inquired, stepping over into the boat and holding out a hand to her.

Ruby hesitated before laying her palm in his, allowing him to assist her into the boat and onto a seat. "I did, thank you. He was only awake for a few minutes, but the doctor said his vitals are strong."

Cranking the boat, the Beast took his seat behind the windshield and motioned for Ruby to stand in front of him.

Her lips stiffened, but she didn't argue. She stood and made her way to the space between him and the boat's wheel.

Lincoln reached around her, pressed his chest against her back, and gripped the wheel.

Her intoxicating scent drifted up his nose, robbing him off breath.

It took enormous effort for him to engage the gear and back the boat out of the boathouse.

He turned east and maneuvered the boat through the rolling waters of the Mississippi, his arms instinctively tightening around her.

"Where are you taking me?" she asked over her shoulder.

Lincoln ignored her, tucking his chin down to keep the hood on his head in place.

The rest of the trip was spent in silence with Lincoln basking in the essence of Ruby.

He pulled up along the bank, grabbed the basket he'd had Mrs. Tuff prepare before he left, and tethered the boat to an old dock that had seen better days.

"We get out here." He extended a hand toward Ruby.

Ruby laid her palm against his, allowing him to help her onto the dock. "What is this place?"

Lincoln wasn't sure why he'd brought Ruby to his quiet place. He often went there when he needed to be alone, to escape from the realities of his life. For some reason, he wanted her to see it.

He wanted her to himself, an inner voice whispered. Away from the staff, from her brother...from everyone but him.

Chapter Twenty-Three

Ruby walked along the dock, nervous and more than a little frightened. Lincoln had taken her quite a distance up the river to a place that looked to be deserted.

She gazed ahead at the small log cabin situated on the bank of the river, and anxiety quickly took hold.

Was he taking her there to hurt her?

Glancing at his cloak-covered back, Ruby said the first thing that came to mind. "Why did you bring me here? If you're going to hurt me, I wish you would tell me. The not knowing is killing me."

Lincoln merely slowed his step and took hold of her hand, forcing her to walk faster. "I didn't bring you here to hurt you, Ruby."

"Then why did you bring me here?"

"To get to know you."

Relief was swift, but short lived. A massive alligator slid from the bank into the water not ten feet from the dock they were on.

Scrambling forward, Ruby all but climbed up Lincoln's back.

He stopped, half turned, and swept her up into his arms. "It's just a gator."

A deep growling sound came from the gator now disappearing beneath the dock.

Ruby bit back a scream, buried her face against Lincoln's neck, and drew her knees up as high as she could get them. There were three things in the world that terrified her: spiders, sharks, and alligators.

Lincoln lifted her higher against his chest and tightened his arms around her. "You're safe now."

She wasn't about to look, not until they were safely inside the cabin.

Ruby snuggled closer. It didn't matter that she was in the arms of the beastlike creature she knew lurked beneath that hood. As long as he kept her from being gator food.

His scent suddenly penetrated her fear, seeping into her senses like a warm summer wind. He smelled incredible, she realized, taking another hesitant breath.

Memories of him caressing her arm in her sleep drifted through her mind. She took another deep breath. How could this beastly creature possess such a gentle touch?

He abruptly lowered her to her feet.

Ruby had been so distracted by the scent of him, she hadn't realized they were inside the cabin.

"If you need to use the bathroom, it's right over there." Lincoln waved a hand toward a door to his right.

Uncomfortable at the direction her thoughts had taken, Ruby cleared her throat and took a step back. "I-I'm fine."

She remained where she was and took in the cabin's interior while Lincoln dusted off the table and set the basket on its surface.

"Are you hungry?" he rasped, opening the basket to retrieve its contents.

Ruby realized she hadn't eaten since earlier that morning. "I could eat."

He pulled out a chair and sat, indicating that she should do the same. "Have a seat."

More than a little nervous, Ruby joined him at the small wooden table.

She watched in silence as he poured them some red wine, unfolded a cloth containing cheese and crackers and then opened a few more containers of fried chicken along with some potato salad.

What he did next shocked her into silence.

His hands slowly lifted to the cloak's button at his neck. He released it and carefully pushed the hood back, slipping the garment free.

Ruby's eyes grew huge. She could do nothing but stare at the inhumane face of the Beast in front of her.

Lincoln didn't blink, only peered at her with those electric blue eyes. "This is who I am. You will eat with this face, spend your days with this face, and sleep with this face. Though I resemble a monster, I am still a man. But I am also a man with needs. And you will meet those needs."

"Now?" Ruby whispered, more in shock than in fear.

The Beast shrugged a massive shoulder. "I haven't decided yet. But I meant what I said. I will not harm, so you can relax. Now, eat."

Ruby swallowed hard. She couldn't force her gaze away from his face. He wasn't as hideous as she'd originally thought.

His hair, a chestnut color, hung loose around his shoulders. Though his forehead was larger than a normal man's, it somehow fit his beastly form. His teeth resembled his timber wolf's, but his bottom lip was full and soft looking. His nose appeared more animal than man, and a light dusting of hair covered his cheeks. But his eyes were what held her attention most. They had to be the bluest she'd ever seen.

"Are you going to stare or eat?" he snapped, snatching up her plate and filling it full of food.

Ruby jumped at his growling tone. "Excuse me, but you're the one who decided to remove the hood. I was merely looking."

His movements were jerky with obvious anger or maybe embarrassment. She couldn't decide.

"Tell me about Spencer."

That caught her off guard. "There's nothing to tell."

"Humor me," he practically snarled, setting her plate back in front of her and filling his own.

Ruby didn't want to discuss Spencer. Especially not with the Beast.

She picked up her fork, took a bite of potato salad, and spoke once she'd swallowed. "I don't know what you want me to say. Spencer and I have been seeing each other since the tenth grade."

"Do you love him?" He took a large bite of his own food.

Ruby thought about that for a moment, remembering the brunette she'd seen in Spencer's room. "I thought I did."

Something flickered in the Beast's eyes. "But you're not sure?"

"I'm not sure of anything anymore." And she meant it. Her entire life had changed over the past week. "May I ask you a question now?"

He only nodded.

"When can I make Daddy's funeral arrangements?"

His expression turned angry. "If it were up to me, I would dump him in the river for the gators to feast on. But since he was your father, I had Templeton make the arrangements. The funeral is in two days. All expenses have been taken care of."

Though it enraged her to hear him speak of her father in such a way, Ruby was too relieved that Lincoln had taken care of the funeral. So, she let his remark slide. "Thank you."

He brushed off her words of thanks. "Tell me about college."

Swallowing her next bite, Ruby wiped her mouth with a napkin. "I have attended the University of California in Berkeley for the last two years. I'm studying to be a vet."

"I see. And how much longer before you receive your degree?"

"Two more years."

The Beast continued to question her around ravenous bites of food. "And if you obtain custody of your brother, how will you manage college then?"

Ruby hadn't thought that far ahead. "I don't know. I suppose I'll have to finish out the year at a local community college and go from there."

Try as she might, she couldn't bring herself to look away from Lincoln's face. He truly was a beast. "May I ask you another question?"

"You may."

"How do you know that you're cursed and this" — she indicated his face — "isn't some birth defect?"

Lincoln stopped chewing and took a long pull from his wineglass. "You've spent the last two years in medical school, Ruby. Have you ever known of a human child born to resemble an animal? A beast?"

"That doesn't mean it can't happen," she weakly responded. "I mean, just because your face is different — "

"My face?" he interrupted, surging to his feet. "You think this curse stops with my face?"

He suddenly reached up, gripped the hem of his shirt, and yanked it over his head. His gloves came off next.

Ruby nearly swallowed her tongue. She'd never seen a chest that size before. Muscles bulged from his shoulders to the waistband of his form-fitting jeans. His stomach was ripped with washboard abs that appeared hard as marble. But his massive, claw-tipped hands were what threw her most.

She quickly glanced away, scared and intrigued all at the same time. "I'm sorry. I didn't mean to imply that it's not true. It's just that, well, you have to understand how hard it is for me to grasp that you were cursed to be a beast."

He pulled his shirt back on and returned to his seat. "Now you know."

And she did know. Something inside her wanted to believe him. *Did* believe him. "And my grandmother did this to you." It wasn't a question.

The Beast leaned back in his chair, his electric blue eyes glowing with intensity. He proceeded to tell Ruby the story of how he came to be.

Chapter Twenty-Four

Lincoln watched Ruby closely as he recited the story of Agatha Atwood's curse and the death of his mother that occurred during childbirth.

He saw moments of fear in her eyes, but never once did she interrupt him or appear as if she didn't believe him.

Throughout the revisiting of his past, his mind continued to stray to the dock when he'd held Ruby in his arms. She had pressed her face against his neck, trusting him to protect her.

She finally held up a hand. "And my father had the means to break this curse?"

"He was aware of it," Lincoln admitted, tearing his thoughts from the memory of Ruby in his arms. "I believe that he did. But as far as I know, that knowledge died with him."

For some reason, Lincoln couldn't bring himself to tell Ruby of the riddle her grandmother had left for him. He much preferred her fear over her pity. And he somehow knew she would pity him.

He abruptly pushed his chair back from the table and removed his shirt once more. "Come here."

Uncertainty flashed in her eyes, but she did as he demanded. She slowly stood and rounded the table, stopping about a foot in front of him.

Lincoln took hold of her hand, gently tugging her forward. "Close your eyes."

Her lids squeezed tightly shut, and a barely noticeable tremor passed through her. Had he not been so in tune with her, he might have missed it.

He brought her hand up to his chest and held it against his skin. "Touch me."

Licking her lips in a way he'd come to associate with her being nervous, she flattened her palm and slowly coasted it up to his neck.

"More," he urged, his own eyes sliding shut.

The feel of her fingers slipping through the fur of his chest had to be the most incredible sensation the Beast had ever felt. In all his twenty-nine years, he'd never felt a female's touch in this capacity.

A moan slipped from his lips.

He jerked his eyes open to find her staring back at him with a look of curiosity on her face. But it was gone so fast he was sure he'd imagined it. "That's enough."

Ruby hurried back to her seat, her face pale and drawn.

"Finish your food."

He noticed her hand trembled as she picked up her fork. He replaced his shirt, hoping to get her talking again. "Tell me about your life."

"My...life?"

Lincoln nodded, averting his gaze. He couldn't bear to see the revulsion he knew would be lurking in her beautiful eyes. "Your favorite foods, music, colors...things like that."

"Um, okay," she hesitantly began. "I love all kinds of food, but my favorite is steak. As for music, I love the blues, anything by Kenny Wayne Shepherd, Jonny Lang, Stevie Ray Vaughan. And my favorite color is silver."

Silver looked amazing on her, Lincoln thought, taking in everything she told him. Hence the reason he'd picked the silver dress and diamonds the night she'd had dinner with him. It simply...fit.

He chanced a peek at her from beneath his lashes, noticing how she fidgeted with her fork.

"Steak is my favorite too." *Where did that come from?*

"Really? Rare, medium, or well done?"

Lincoln answered without thinking. "Rare."

Her eyes widened slightly. "Is that because you're a...um, I mean..."

"I know what you meant," he snapped, regretting it instantly when she shrank back.

She dropped her gaze to her plate. "I didn't mean any insult. Sometimes, I speak without carefully thinking my words through. My daddy always said that I lacked a filter."

The mention of Charles Atwood served only to anger Lincoln more.

"I really am sorry," she mumbled, laying her fork aside.

Lincoln brushed off her apology and nodded toward her plate. "Are you finished?"

"I'm not that hungry. But the food was good."

He abruptly stood. "Come, I want to show you something."

"Outside?" She glanced skittishly at the door.

Lincoln's lips almost twitched. Almost. "Alligators usually only attack if you are near their nest. And we are going in the opposite direction."

"Usually?" Ruby rose from her chair. "This will probably be one of those *unusual* times."

The Beast studied her nervous stature.

He moved up next to her and bent his knees. "Get on."

"Your back?"

The uncertainty in her voice wasn't lost on him.

"Yes, my back!" he snapped, leaning down a little lower.

Ruby jumped at his words and stepped onto her chair to wrap her arms around his neck and climb onto his back.

Lincoln immediately hooked his forearms under her knees, lifting her higher.

The feel of her small body pressed firmly against his back did strange things to Lincoln's insides. And then her scent hit him again.

A growl of desire rose in his throat, but he swallowed it back. The last thing he wanted was for her to see the attraction he felt for her.

Though it killed him to admit it to himself, Lincoln recognized the attraction he had for Ruby. Hard as he tried to fight it, the feeling only seemed to grow with every minute they spent together.

It angered him that he wanted her. She was the enemy. The spawn of Charles Atwood.

She climbed up higher on his back the moment he stepped out the door. Lincoln was lost.

"Where are we going?" she questioned, her warm breath fanning his ear.

Lincoln stomped toward the back of the cabin, attempting to think of anything but the sweet scent of the girl clinging to his back. "To my mother's garden. Father had this cabin built for her before I was born. I'm told that she came here a lot when she wanted to be alone."

"Do you have any brothers or sisters?"

"No. My father never remarried." Reaching his destination, the Beast bent at the knees to allow Ruby to slide off his back.

She merely climbed up higher. "Are you sure there are no gators back here?"

A strangled sound burst from his throat, half growl, half chuckle.

The Beast stilled, caught off guard by the emotion. It was the first time in his life he'd ever laughed.

Chapter Twenty-Five

Ruby glanced around at the surrounding area. Woods covered both sides of the small cabin, providing dozens of places for alligators to hide.

She realized that Lincoln had lowered her toward the ground, but there was no way in hades her feet were touching earth until he could assure her that no gators lurked about.

Was that a laugh she'd heard coming from him? "You can think it's funny all you want, but I'm not coming down."

Another odd sound came from him. It took her a moment to realize his upper body shook with laughter, and another for her to join in.

Whether she laughed from nerves or from the insanely comical situation she found herself in, Ruby couldn't stop the chuckle that spilled forth.

And there, behind the small rundown cabin on the banks of the Mississippi, an unlikely bond was formed between two very different souls.

They laughed until Lincoln dropped to his knees and Ruby unwittingly slipped off his back.

I must be crazy, she thought, wiping the tears of mirth from her eyes. *I'm in the woods with a Beast that can't possibly be human, finding humor in a situation that's so far from funny, it's insane.*

The Beast sobered first. "I do not know where that came from. I have never laughed like that before."

"It's been a long time for me as well," Ruby admitted, pushing to her feet while immediately checking her surroundings again. "What is it that you wanted to show me?"

Lincoln stood also, gesturing toward a clearing up ahead. "Would you prefer to be carried?"

"I think I can make it. I suppose if we were going to be eaten, it would have happened by now."

His electric blue eyes twinkled. "I suppose you're right."

Ruby followed him toward the clearing, her breath catching as a multitude of different colored rose bushes came into view, enclosed inside an old wrought iron fence. "Wow, it's beautiful. Did you do this?"

He shook his head. "My mother started it before I was born, but I've kept it up since I was old enough to come here alone."

Something shifted inside Ruby. She peered over at Lincoln's profile. He'd grown up alone, an outcast cursed from birth. A boy who had never known a mother's love. "My brother grew up without a mother also."

Lincoln stiffened. The relaxed look on his face turned hard. "You think to compare me to your brother?"

"No. I—"

"We are nothing alike," he growled turning to face her. "Millions of children grow up without mothers. But only one was cursed to live as a beast. Me!"

He spun on his heel and strode back toward the cabin, leaving Ruby to run in order to catch up.

"I'm sorry," Ruby breathed, stepping into the cabin behind him. "I didn't mean to sound insensitive."

Gathering up the picnic paraphernalia, Lincoln kept his back to her. "Your pity is neither wanted nor needed."

Helplessness welled up inside Ruby. No matter what she said or did, she always seemed to offend him. "I don't pity you, you big jerk! I just thought that if we were going to be spending the next three weeks together, maybe, just maybe we could get along."

Lincoln turned with basket in hand. "Let's get back. I have much to do before it gets dark."

Ruby stepped to the side as he came barreling past her. He stormed down the hill to the dock, leaving her to fend for herself where the gators were concerned.

* * * *

Ruby entered Cameron's room, careful not to wake him. After spending a tense ride back in the boat with Lincoln, her nerves couldn't handle the pain her brother was sure to be in when he woke.

"Has he come to yet?" she asked the nurse, busying herself on the opposite side of Cameron's bed.

The nurse gently smiled. "For a minute. The pain meds we have him on pretty much keep him sedated. He drifts in and out."

"So, he's not in any pain?"

"Nothing unbearable," the nurse assured her. "I'll just go out and give you some time alone with him."

Ruby returned her smile. "Thank you."

Once the nurse disappeared into the hallway, Ruby sat in a chair next to Cameron's bed and took hold of his hand.

"Hi, Cam," she whispered softly. "I know you can't hear me. I just needed to talk to you."

Taking a shuddering breath, she kissed the back of his small hand and continued. "I'm sorry I wasn't there when you were hurt. And I'm also sorry that I haven't been around for the last couple of days. But I'm doing everything I can to make sure that you are taken care of."

Swallowing against the lump in her throat, Ruby blinked back the tears that threatened to choke her. "You're going to be okay, Cam. I promise. You'll be back in your own room very soon, and I'll even get you the new video game you've been asking for."

Ruby paused, her next words seemingly pulled from her very soul. "Daddy will no longer be with us, Cam, but I promise you that I'll do everything in my power to make sure you're happy. I'll even move to a local college, so I can be home with you every night."

Kissing his hand once more, Ruby rubbed his palm against the side of her face. "I know I haven't always been the best sister, and I'm sorry for that. I love you, Cameron. I love you with all my heart, and I would trade places with you in a second if I could."

With a heavy heart, Ruby returned his arm to his side and rested her chin on the railing of his bed to watch him sleep.

He looked so young and pale, lying there helpless with tubes running from every direction.

She thought of Lincoln and wondered what he'd looked like as a child, how alone he must have felt. He'd had no mother to hold his hand when he hurt, no sister to tell him that everything would be all right. *How utterly lonely he must have been.*

Chapter Twenty-Six

Lincoln stood in the hallway, holding his breath, listening to Ruby talk to her brother.

Something inside him shifted, the longer he remained there taking in her heartfelt words.

The Beast had never had anyone speak to him in such a way. He'd never known the tender touch of another, never experienced the unconditional love that Ruby obviously felt for her brother.

He leaned heavily against the wall, unable to pull himself away from the whispered words pouring from her lips.

A deep-rooted anger quickly rose up to replace the longing he felt clawing at his insides.

Curse her for making him feel, and curse him for allowing her under his skin.

Lincoln Barone had spent his entire life perfecting the art of solitude. He preferred being alone, found comfort in the things he enjoyed, such as his timber wolf, Loki, his cabin in the woods, and his mother's roses.

But that was before Ruby Atwood waltzed into his life and disrupted his peace of mind.

Granted, he'd manipulated her there and blackmailed her into staying. But he hadn't counted on caring for her.

He wanted to dislike her, had been conditioned to resent her since the day he'd heard about her birth, yet now that he had her in his grasp, he could do nothing but obsess over her.

Pushing away from the wall, Lincoln staggered back toward the stairs and into the safety of his bedroom. But everywhere he went, her scent seemed to haunt him.

He snatched up her clothes that lay across the vanity bench and tossed them across the room before wandering over to the glass-covered rose that sat next to the window.

The last petal had wilted and would fall within a matter of weeks. He wanted to jerk up the glass and rip the idiotic petal free. It was nothing but a constant reminder of what he would never have…what he would always be.

"What is that for?"

Ruby's quietly spoken question caught him off guard. He'd been so wrapped up in his anger he hadn't heard her come up the stairs.

He turned to face her. "What do you want?"

"Why is there a dead rose beneath that glass?" she persisted, inching into the room.

Lincoln wanted to rail at her that it was her dead grandmother's way of tormenting him. But instead, he said, "How is your brother?"

"He's sleeping. The nurse said he was getting stronger, and that the sleep helps him heal." She trailed farther into the room. "Why are you avoiding my question about the rose?"

Lincoln lifted the hood of his cloak, noticing that she didn't shrink back from his beastly appearance. "It's part of my curse. When the last petal falls, it seals my fate."

"Your fate?" She stopped before him.

"This." He lifted his hand to indicate his face. "I will remain this way until my death."

Ruby shifted her gaze to the glass case. "Is there no way to break the curse?"

"No way humanly possible," Lincoln practically snarled. "Your grandmother made sure of that."

Though Ruby flinched from his tone, she didn't retreat. "Tell me."

"There's nothing to tell."

She took a step closer and reached up to touch his face. "I think there is."

Lincoln jerked back, horrified of what she'd intended to do. "Don't."

"I can touch your chest but not your face?"

The thought of her soft, perfect hand coming into contact with his hideous face horrified him.

He shook his head and changed the subject. "Dinner will be ready soon. If you would like to change, there are plenty of dresses in the armoire. I'll leave you to it." With that, he brushed past her and strode from the room.

The doorbell rang as Lincoln descended the stairs. He lifted his hood to cover his head and opened the door.

Spencer Wright stood on the porch. "I'm looking for Ruby Atwood."

Lincoln felt as if he'd been kicked in the gut, so great was his shock. How dare the arrogant Spencer show up on his doorstep, asking after what belonged to Lincoln.

And Ruby did belong to him. Even if he had to blackmail her for the rest of her life to keep her there. He would never allow her to leave him now.

"You have the wrong house." He moved to shut the door.

The unwanted idiot quickly lodged his foot in it. "I know she's here. You either let me speak with her, or —"

"Spencer?" Ruby called out on her way down the stairs. "I thought that was your voice I heard."

She came to a stop next to Lincoln and pulled the door wider. "What are you doing here?"

"Looking for you."

An uncontrollable rage began to simmer in Lincoln's chest.

Ruby somehow wedged herself between Lincoln and the door, her attention focused on

Spencer. "How did you know where to find me?"

"Mrs. Fleming told me where you would be."

The Beast opened his mouth to threaten Spencer's life, but Ruby's next words stopped him.

"She had no right to tell you that. Leave here, Spencer. And never come back." She slammed the door in his face.

Lincoln's heart stuttered. Ruby had just run Spencer off without batting an eye.

He stared down at her serene face, unable to voice his feelings.

She calmly looked up at him as if nothing untoward had just happened. "We should hurry and get dressed, or we'll be late for dinner."

The Beast stood there slack mouthed long after she marched up the stairs and disappeared from view.

He couldn't seem to move, his entire body tense with an emotion he'd never experienced before. Was he falling in love with Ruby?

Panic settled in to replace his shock. He couldn't love her; he wouldn't allow it. She could never return his feelings, never care for someone as hideous as him. No, Ruby Atwood was far too beautiful and kind to love a beast.

Chapter Twenty-Seven

Ruby numbly showered and changed into a pretty blue summer dress she'd found hanging in the armoire.

The Beast would like it, she decided, slipping on a soft pair of white sandals.

Picking up the brush, she paused in bringing it to her hair. Had she really just dressed to please Lincoln Barone, the man who'd blackmailed her into selling herself to him?

Only, he hadn't actually forced her to be intimate with him, she silently admitted. And he could have, numerous times.

She wondered what it would be like to surrender to him. Would it disgust her? Would he make her do things that she didn't want to do? Would he hurt her?

Another question cropped up in her mind. Why hadn't he consummated their arrangement? Did he not find her good enough for him? With his money, he probably had hundreds of women on the side. Women that cared more about his finances than his looks.

For some reason that thought bothered her.

Suddenly insecure, she sat on the edge of his bed, imagining him with dozens of faceless women.

Shaking off her disturbing thoughts, she moved to stand when her gaze landed on a blanket covering something near the head of the bed.

Without thinking, she reached up and tugged the blanket free.

"A mirror?" she whispered, shocked to find one in his room. It was first one she'd seen in the house since her arrival.

The long, oval-shaped mirror was trimmed in what looked to be antique wood. It would be gorgeous if not for the broken piece of glass along the bottom.

"What are you doing with that?" Lincoln growled, striding into the room with his hood in place. The door slammed shut behind him.

For some reason, Ruby wasn't afraid. "Just looking at it. I thought you didn't like mirrors."

"I don't," he shot back, yanking the blanket from her hands. "This particular one was another torturous gift from Agatha Atwood."

Ruby's stomach flipped. "My grandmother gave it to you? But why?"

"As I said, to torture me with."

"I don't understand," Ruby persisted, wishing more than anything that she could see his expression.

Lincoln stilled for long moments, standing in front of her with that blanket in his hand. "I will show you, but you have to do something for me in return."

More curious than afraid, Ruby slowly nodded. "Okay, what?"

"Allow me to touch you."

Her heart stuttered. A blush spread up her neck into her face. Though she'd known this moment would come, she wasn't sure if she was ready for it. She shifted uncomfortably.

Lincoln moved to cover the mirror.

"Wait," Ruby breathed, reaching up to stop him. "Okay. Just please don't hurt me."

He stiffened beneath her touch, but didn't bite her head off. And with those teeth, Ruby never doubted he could.

Dropping the covering, the Beast pulled the mirror over, stopping directly in front of Ruby. He then threw his leg up onto the bed, slid around behind her, and straddled her from the back.

Ruby watched in the mirror as he reached up and pushed the hood back off his head. His eyes were closed, but the man in the reflection in front of her definitely couldn't be Lincoln Barone.

"Oh my God," she whispered, her heart pounding erratically. "Impossible."

His hair resembled that of the Beast's, but that was where the similarities ended. The man she saw in the mirror had to be one of the most beautiful men Ruby had ever laid eyes on.

Unable to wrap her mind around what was happening, Ruby turned her head slightly to see the Beast sitting behind her.

She shifted her stunned gaze back to his reflection, only to suck in a startled breath when he leaned in closer and opened his eyes.

"It *is* you!" There, staring intently at her from over her shoulder, were those same electric blue eyes she'd seen earlier on the Beast.

Her gaze dropped to his mouth, and what a mouth he had. Full, sensual, and resting close to her ear.

"What… This is… How?" she stammered, her gaze devouring his handsome face.

"I don't know how, Ruby. I only know that Agatha sent it to me. I assume it was to torment me with what might have been, would have been, had I not been cursed."

Ruby couldn't seem to look away. "This is what you were meant to look like."

"I can handle anything but your pity, Ruby. Do not pity me."

Ruby blinked. She hadn't meant to show him pity.

"Release your hair from its restraint."

Heat rushed to her face. "May I at least shut the curtains? It's awfully bright in here."

"I want to see you. All of you. Every expression, every freckle."

That sent her gaze elsewhere. She couldn't bring herself to look at him given what she was about to do.

Taking an unsteady breath, Ruby lifted her arms and freed her hair.

She could hear the Beast's uneven breathing, feel his shuttering breaths next to her ear. It took everything she had not to run.

"Beautiful. You are the most beautiful creature, I have ever beheld.

More heat traveled through her.

Ruby had never thought herself beautiful. Passable, maybe, but never beautiful.

She found herself relaxing under his attention.

His hands softly came around her to rest on her abdomen. He gently pulled her back against him and brought his lips to her ear. "Relax. I won't hurt you."

Ruby noticed his hands shook. She hesitantly lifted her gaze, surprised to find him staring back at her, devouring her with those electric blue eyes.

Something in his touch melted her insides. She couldn't look away from him, even with his next whispered words.

"Put your arms around my neck."

She lifted her arms without question, looping them around his neck.

His blue eyes slid shut. "Touch me, Ruby."

Ruby slid her fingers into his long, chestnut-colored hair and coasted her palms along his scalp.

A moan slipped from his full lips. "Again."

She shyly massaged his head and neck, watching in fascination as his expression changed from pleasure to bliss.

It made her feel powerful. She shifted between his jean-clad legs, pushing back against his body heat.

"Ah, Ruby…" Lincoln's hands inched up her ribs, the pads of his fingers stroking soft circles across her skin.

Ruby experienced her own moan as he nuzzled the side of her face with his cheek.

Her eyes closed of their own volition. She found herself lost in sensations she'd never imagined possible.

Of all the times she and Spencer had kissed and held each other, Ruby had never experienced the level of feelings she now felt in Lincoln's arms.

Maybe it was the mirror, or perhaps her grandmother's curse that seduced her in that moment. Whatever the reason, it had to be the most powerful sensation Ruby had ever felt. And she didn't want it to end.

She tightened her hold on Lincoln's head and slowly turned her face toward his suddenly close lips.

A low growl rumbled from his chest. It vibrated against her, adding to her urge to kiss him. Ruby was lost.

Chapter Twenty-Eight

Lincoln's body shook with a mixture of disbelief and need. Ruby was touching him.

The Beast within him warred with the man in the mirror. Take her, the Beast demanded, fighting to be unleashed. But the man inside, resisted. "I'll hurt you, Ruby. If we don't stop this now, I *will* hurt you."

A knock sounded on the bedroom door. "Miss Atwood?"

The arrival of his housekeeper couldn't have come at a better time, thought Lincoln.

Ruby stilled, her gaze flying toward the door. "Yes, Mrs. Tuff?"

"Your brother is awake. He's asking for you."

Ruby's soft gasp echoed throughout the otherwise quiet room. "I have to go."

Lincoln held completely still, unable to move for fear of yanking her back and finishing what they'd started.

She jumped from the bed and turned to face him. Her mouth opened without sound.

Lincoln couldn't bear the look on her face. He quickly lifted his hood in place and stood as well. "Go."

Ruby nodded and left without another word.

Stumbling to the bathroom, Lincoln turned on the water to the sink and splashed some of the cool liquid onto his overheated face.

Ruby had touched him.

A vision of her in Wright's arms drifted through Lincoln's mind. Did she enjoy being with Spencer? Did she enjoy his touch as much as she'd seemed to enjoy Lincoln's?

He gripped the sink's edge, frustrated and angry at the situation.

No matter, he decided, taking a deep breath of resolve. He would keep Ruby with him, even if he had to spend the rest of his days simply holding her in his arms.

* * * *

Lincoln took a seat at the head of the table and thanked Mrs. Tuff for making dinner.

Obviously shocked by his display of manners, she blinked at him, a comical look on her made-up face. "Are you feeling all right, Mr. Barone?"

"I'm fine, Mrs. Tuff. Have you let Ruby know that it's dinner time yet?"

"Yes, sir. She will be right in. She was holding her brother's hand while he dozed off to sleep."

A spark of jealousy settled in Lincoln's gut. He'd give anything for Ruby to love him with the same fierceness she loved her brother.

"Am I too late?" Ruby trailed into the room, looking more beautiful than ever. Though her eyes appeared tired.

The Beast stood and pulled out her chair. "You're just in time."

Ruby sat and waited for Lincoln to return to his chair. "Would you mind removing your hood? I'd like to be able to see your eyes if we are going to converse during dinner."

Lincoln stilled. "You want to look at my face while you eat?"

"I've seen it before. You're not as scary as you'd like to think," she attempted to tease, picking up the glass of wine in front of her.

Unsure of whether to remove the hood and risk turning her stomach, Lincoln sat there until she leaned over and made the decision for him.

"There, that's better," she stated, pulling the hood from his head.

Lincoln met her beautiful gaze. "It really doesn't bother you to be subjected to…this?" He lifted a hand and indicated his face.

Ruby took a sip of her wine. "You're different, Lincoln. But I see something inside you that I don't think you see."

Lincoln looked away, afraid she would pick up on the emotion he so desperately tried to hide.

For reasons he would never understand, Ruby didn't run screaming from the room when subjected to his beastly features. She looked at him as if he were perfectly normal, as if he were actually a…man.

Chapter Twenty-Nine

Ruby spent the next two weeks in a haze of grief and confusion.

She'd buried her father not long after Cameron's arrival at the Barone mansion. Lincoln had even allowed her to hold a memorial on the grounds, where Cameron could say his goodbyes.

Some of Charles's friends had attended the memorial, most with suspicious eyes and questions that Ruby couldn't answer.

How was she to tell them her reasons for being at the Barone mansion without inviting accusations? Though, in a nutshell that was exactly what she deserved. She had, after all, allowed him to blackmail her into being there.

But Barone hadn't forced her to be with him. Every night, he would crawl into bed beside her, roll her to her side, and pull her back against his front.

He hadn't touched her intimately since the one time in front of the very mirror she sat in front of now.

Ruby knew he wanted her. The evidence of his need shone from his eyes every night before she fell asleep in his arms.

She peered at her reflection, wondering what had changed since he'd touched her with such tenderness.

And if she were being completely honest with herself, she would admit to wanting him to do it again.

Maybe it had to do with the fact that Lincoln was unlike any man she'd ever known before.

But he's not a man, her mind whispered. *He's a beast.*

"Excuse me, miss?"

Ruby started at the sound of Mrs. Tuff's voice. She'd been so wrapped up in thoughts of Lincoln, she hadn't heard the housekeeper's approach. "Yes?"

"There's a Mrs. Goodson from the Department of Children and Families here to see you."

Anxiety quickly replaced Ruby's earlier musings. She surged to her feet. "The DCF worker? How the world did she know I would be here?"

"I don't know, miss. But she sure isn't a friendly one."

Ruby slipped on her shoes and hurried toward the door where Mrs. Tuff stood. "Where is she?"

The housekeeper jerked her thumb toward the direction of the stairs. "In Cameron's room."

"What? Where's Lincoln?"

Mrs. Tuff shrugged. "I haven't seen him in over an hour. I figured he was gearing up for the anticipated Hurricane Walter."

Ruby wondered why he'd left without telling her, but decided she'd think about that later. Right now, she had a DCF worker to deal with. "Let's pray that hurricane bypasses us."

Descending the stairs, Ruby quickly freed her hair from its ponytail and ran her fingers through it. She straightened her shirt, cleared her throat, and entered Cameron's room. "Mrs. Goodson. You wanted to see me?"

The short, plump redhaired social worker sat in a chair next to Cameron's bed, holding some sort of ledger in her hands. She scrawled something on one of the lines before lifting her gaze to Ruby. "I did. We received a call that Mr. Barone requested temporary guardianship of Cameron as a means to force you here. Can you tell me how long you have been staying here with Mr. Barone and what your relationship to him is?"

Ruby's mouth dropped open. "I don't see what my relationship with Mr. Barone has to do with my custody case."

"Actually, it has a lot to do with it." The social worker sniffed. "Especially if the accusations are true. Were you coerced into to coming here?"

"Of course not." Ruby balked, taking a nervous step closer. "Where did you hear something like that?" But she knew. Spencer Wright was definitely responsible.

Mrs. Goodson snapped her ledger closed and stood. "I'm not at liberty to say. All callers are kept confidential, and any information obtained through those calls may be used in our investigation. Now, would you mind showing me where you sleep?"

Ruby's stomach dropped. If Mrs. Goodson found that she'd been sleeping in Lincoln's room, it would only cement the accusations that Ruby had been coerced.

Panicked, Ruby said the first thing that came to mind. "I sleep with my fiancé."

Mrs. Goodson raised an eyebrow. "And who is your fiancé?"

"I am," Lincoln answered, stepping into the room.

Ruby spun to face a cloak-covered Lincoln, shock and relief both scrambling for dominance. She immediately moved to his side and leaned heavily against him.

The social worker backed up a step, her head tilting back to peer up at Lincoln's hooded face. "And you are?"

"Lincoln Barone," he rasped, moving in closer to tower over the woman. "My attorney has been notified of your bullying tactics where my fiancée is concerned. He's on the phone with the judge as we speak. I highly doubt you will have a job by the day's end. Now, I'd appreciate it if you would get out of my house."

Mrs. Goodson's round, plump face reddened with rage. She gathered her things and marched toward the door. "We'll just see about that."

Ruby threw her arms around Lincoln the second Mrs. Goodson stomped from the room.

"You're trembling," he acknowledged, returning her hug.

Safe, Ruby thought, squeezing him tighter. He made her feel safe. "She's going to cause me to lose my brother, Lincoln. I just know it."

"I won't allow that."

Ruby snuggled closer. "But I told her that you were my fiancé. What if the judge sees it as a ploy on my part to help my custody case?"

"You have to trust me, Ruby. Your hearing is in three days. Everything will be all right."

She backed up a step to gaze into his shadowed face. "How can you be so sure?"

Lincoln shrugged a massive shoulder. "I just am."

Ruby frowned, wondering how he could be so certain about the outcome of her hearing. "This is my brother we're talking about. I can't lose him, Lincoln."

"He's safe here. You both are. I feel that this is the best place for you to be right now. Regardless of the social worker's accusations. Only…"

"Only what?" Ruby whispered, studying his solemn expression.

"Your hearing is the day before my birthday," Lincoln informed her, a certain sadness in his eyes. "I don't think it's wise for you to be here for that."

Understanding dawned. "Your curse."

He nodded. "I don't know what will happen on that day. When the clock strikes midnight, signaling my birthday, this curse will forever be my fate. If something happens inside me, something darker and more unnatural, I'd rather you and Cameron not be around to witness it."

"I understand how you feel, Lincoln, but if something does happen to you on that night, I can't think of anywhere else I'd rather be than by your side. You'll need a friend."

Chapter Thirty

Lincoln felt as if his stomach had dropped to his shoes. On the one hand, Ruby had offered to stay, to see him through his thirtieth birthday and the unknown that would accompany it. But she would be there only as a friend.

What had he expected? Did he really think that Ruby would see past his beastly form and profess her undying love for him?

The Beast had absorbed her laughter, her caresses, sweet words of comfort, and held them close to his heart. But he knew deep down that it was time to let her go. She would never love him...not in the way he yearned to be loved.

Ruby Atwood was beautiful. She could have any man she wanted. And she needed a man. Not some beast who could never give her the life she deserved.

He took her by the hand and guided her from the room. "I'm surprised Cameron slept through the social worker's visit."

"Me too," Ruby confessed, clinging tightly to Lincoln's hand. "Especially with that nasally, high-pitched voice she has."

Lincoln's lips twitched.

"What you said to her back there. Was that true?"

"About her not having a job to return to?"

At Ruby's nod, he continued. "Yes. She has no business working with children or families. People such as her are power hungry. They get off on wielding that power over the weaker. Makes me sick."

"Thank you for coming to my rescue back there, Lincoln. I'm sorry, I threw you under the bus with that fiancé comment, but it was the first thing that popped into my mind."

Lincoln wanted to yank her to him and assure her that she hadn't thrown him under anything he didn't want to be under. That he would give anything to be normal, to be her fiancé.

Instead, he said. "It's fine. You did what had to be done. I don't fault you for that."

"I'd like to go for a swim in the pool while Cam's asleep," Ruby suddenly announced, catching Lincoln off guard. "Join me?"

The thought of Ruby seeing his face outside in the bright light of day didn't appeal to Lincoln. But the pleading look in her eyes decided for him. "Sure."

Ruby grinned. "Great. Grab yourself some shorts, and I'll meet you out there."

Lincoln didn't own a pair of shorts. He'd never had a need for them, but he didn't want to tell Ruby that. "Okay. Give me a few minutes."

He waited for her to trail off toward the back of the giant house before taking the stairs two at a time to the second floor.

Mrs. Tuff turned from her dusting of a table in the hall as he rushed toward his bedroom. "Is everything okay, Mr. Barone?"

Lincoln stopped just inside his room and spun to face her. "I need a pair of shorts. And quickly."

The housekeeper's eyebrows shot up. "Shorts, Mr. Barone?"

"Yes. Something to swim in. And please hurry. Ruby's waiting."

Mrs. Tuff smiled knowingly. "Hand me a pair of your jeans, and I'll cut them off for you."

Lincoln retrieved a pair of his jeans from his closet and handed them to her.

"I'll have them to you in a jiffy." Mrs. Tuff bustled from the room with a spring in her step.

Removing his cloak, Lincoln pulled off his shirt, removed his shoes, and peeled off his pants. He stood in the middle of his room in his boxer briefs.

Grabbing a towel, he wrapped it around his waist to save Mrs. Tuff the embarrassment of catching him in his underwear.

The phone rang from his bedside table. Lincoln picked it up and brought it to his ear. He opened his mouth to speak when Mrs. Tuff's voice came over the line. "Barone residence."

"Hi, Virginia, it's Stiles."

Mrs. Tuff practically purred. "Well, hello there, sweetie. Why are you calling the house phone?"

"I tried your cell," he replied with a touch of impatience in his voice. "I'm at the market, and I forgot my list. Can you give me a quick rundown on what you wanted me to pick up?"

Lincoln was about to hang up when Mrs. Tuff's next words stopped him. "I will, but you'll never believe what I'm doing at the moment."

"Are you going to tell me or make me guess?"

The housekeeper's feminine giggle grated on the Beast's nerves. "I'm making Lincoln a pair of shorts. He's going in the pool with Miss Atwood."

"Without his covering?" Stiles sounded as shocked as Lincoln felt by hearing them discuss him in such a manner.

"Yes, poor thing." Mrs. Tuff clucked. "It's kind of sad, if you ask me. The girl obviously pities him, and I don't think Mr. Barone can see it. He seems pretty taken with her."

All the air left Lincoln's lungs in a whoosh. He quietly replaced the receiver and dropped his great weight onto the edge of his bed.

How could he have been so naïve? Mrs. Tuff was more than right. Lincoln had been so caught up in Ruby and how she made him feel that he hadn't been able to see the forest for the trees.

Ruby pitied him. He should have known that was the case the first time she'd allowed him to touch her.

Lincoln couldn't summon the will to be angry. It was no more than he deserved. How stupid he'd been to actually expect someone as beautiful and precious as Ruby to feel anything for him other than pity.

Loki whimpered from the doorway, obviously sensing his master's pain. He trotted into the room, licking Lincoln's hand before laying his head on his thigh.

"Good boy," Lincoln praised him, petting the top of the animal's head.

Lincoln raised his gaze to the cursed mirror in front of him and took in his handsome appearance.

A bone-deep sorrow settled inside him the longer he peered at his reflection. In three days' time, his hope of ever being the man staring back at him would disappear.

Loki whined again.

"It's okay, boy," Lincoln assured him in a soft tone. "Go lay down."

The wolf meandered over to the rug near the foot of the bed and lowered his giant body.

Lincoln wasn't sure how long he sat there, hidden by the partially closed canopy of his bed, when Ruby's voice penetrated his tormented thoughts.

"Lincoln?"

Loki growled low in his throat.

Lincoln snatched up his cloak, threw it over his shoulders, and covered his hideous head.

"What are you doing sitting in here in the dark?" Ruby softly questioned, ignoring the wolf's growls. "Is everything all right?"

Lincoln's stomach tightened in dread. He couldn't face her. Not now. Not after he'd acted like a lovesick fool. He'd never be able to bear the pity he knew would be evident in her eyes.

"I'm fine. Get out."

She took another step forward. "Not until I know that you're okay.

"I said, get out!" he roared, swinging his hooded gaze in her direction.

But there was no pity swimming in her beautiful eyes...only determination.

Chapter Thirty-One

Ruby's heart pounded hard enough she could swear her shirt lifted with every beat. Lincoln was furious. But why? Her gaze swung to the wolf protecting its owner.

Though Loki continued with the growling, Ruby knew enough about animals to know that he wouldn't attack her. He would already be on his feet if that were the case.

She inched forward on trembling legs. "I'm not leaving. Not until you tell me what I've done to anger you."

"You didn't do anything," Lincoln rasped, shrinking farther back into the shadow of the bed's canopy.

She took another step. "Then why are you sitting in here in the shadows? I waited a half hour for you to join me in the pool. It's starting to grow dark out."

"Don't come any closer."

Ruby could hear the anger in his voice along with something else she couldn't identify.

She stopped in front of him, moving to stand between his bare knees. "I'm not leaving until you tell me what's wrong."

He jerked back when she reached up to remove his hood. "I don't want your pity!"

Ruby sucked in a shocked breath. "My pity? You think I pity you?"

"Why else would you still be here?" he bit out, gripping her wrists to prevent her from removing his hood.

Loki surged to his feet, but one word from Lincoln, and the animal turned and left the room.

Tears of frustration burned Ruby's eyes, but she blinked them back. How was she expected to answer his question when she herself wasn't sure why she'd remained?

"I don't know why I'm still here, Lincoln." She tried to wriggle her wrists free of his grasp. "I only know that I can't bring myself to leave. Not yet."

His head slowly lifted. And though she couldn't see his face, she knew he watched her with those electric blue eyes. "Why? What are you waiting for?"

"I don't know. I…"

He tightened his hold. "Tell me!"

"I can't leave," she whispered, yanking free of his hold. "Not until I know what it feels like to have your skin against mine. To lie in your arms, while you take me to a place I've never —
"

"Ruby?"

"Touch me, Lincoln."

"If I touch you now," he rasped, holding still as a statue, "I won't be able to stop."

His words lit a fire inside Ruby that threatened to burn her alive. "Then don't stop."

Lincoln's soft intake of breath echoed throughout the dimly lit room.

He gripped her by the hips, spun her around, and pulled her back against his chest.

Ruby lifted her gaze to the mirror in front of her, lost in a haze of wonder.

Lincoln pushed back the hood of his cloak. Those electric blue eyes burned with a passion as hot as her own. "Run, Ruby. I'm barely clinging to my control."

"I don't want your control, Lincoln. I want you. All of you."

He leaned down until his lips brushed against her ear, his erratic breathing heating the side of her neck. "Please don't tell me to stop."

Stop? Ruby thought in a daze. She wouldn't stop him now if the house was on fire.

Looking into his handsome face, his gorgeous blue eyes, Ruby knew one thing for certain. It was Lincoln she wanted to give herself to. All of him. Not just the beautiful man staring back at her from the mirror, but also the Beast behind her who remained in the shadows.

Ruby suddenly stood. It almost broke her heart to see his devastated reflection, to hear his choked moan of disappointment.

She slowly turned in his arms and lifted her hands to touch his face.

He jerked back in horror. "What are you doing?"

Ruby ignored his desperate attempt to prevent her from touching him and climbed onto his lap. "I want you, Lincoln. Not just the man in the mirror, but *you*."

Brushing the half-askew cloak from his shoulders, Ruby laid her palms against his cheek. "Kiss me."

"Ruby…" he choked out, tears gathering in his soulful blue eyes.

Ruby couldn't hold back her own tears. She allowed them to fall, to bare herself to him, not just in body, but in soul as well. "Please, kiss me."

Lincoln hesitantly leaned down until his mouth hovered an inch above hers, his entire body trembling beneath her.

She could feel his hot breath on her face, smell his amazing scent. "Please…"

With that one tear sparkling on his lashes, Lincoln closed the gap between them and softly brushed her lips with his.

Ruby was lost.

Chapter Thirty-Two

Lincoln's heart shattered into a thousand pieces the moment Ruby touched his face. But nothing prepared him for the tears of surrender in her eyes or the feel of her lips moving beneath his.

He loved her, loved her so much he realized he'd die without her.

She deepened the kiss, wringing another moan from his pain-filled chest. The pain was real. A reminder that he couldn't keep her, that this one night with her would have to last him a lifetime.

"What's wrong?" Ruby asked, breaking off the kiss.

As much as the Beast hated to admit it to her, he owed her his honesty. "I have never been with a woman before."

More tears filled Ruby's eyes. "I'm a virgin too, Lincoln."

Lincoln stilled, not sure he'd heard her right. "What did you say?"

She didn't look away in feigned embarrassment. No coy remarks left her lips. Her gaze softened even more. "You are my first, Lincoln."

His heart began to slam against his ribs. Not only had Ruby freely offered herself to him, but she was giving him the most precious gift a woman could give...her innocence.

Humbled to the point of breaking, Lincoln reached up and cupped the side of her face. "Why, Ruby? Why me?"

"Don't think, Lincoln. Just love me."

* * * *

Ruby snuggled close to Lincoln's side, basking in the afterglow of the most amazing night of her life.

A yawn quickly overtook her. "You know the hurricane that's been swirling out in the gulf?"

"Mmmm," Lincoln responded, pulling her more firmly against him.

"I heard on the radio while I was in the pool that it's taken a turn and is heading this way."

He kissed her on the forehead. "How long before it's expected?"

"Three days, tops." Ruby's eyes grew heavy with sleep.

"I'll need to make more preparations. Is it still a category two?"

Ruby fought another yawn, her eyes slowly closing. "According to the weather channel, it is, but it could strengthen with landfall."

"But your court date—"

"Is first thing Thursday morning. The hurricane, *if* it hits here, isn't due to land until late Thursday night."

"I don't like the idea of you being in the city that close to the time of the storm."

Ruby kissed him on the shoulder. "I won't be. I'll be back long before the rain even starts. Besides, it'll give me a chance to check on things at home."

Lincoln stiffened. She felt the moment he emotionally withdrew from her.

What had she said that would warrant such a reaction? "Did I say something wrong?"

He only shook his head. "You should get some sleep. I'm sure you have a lot to do tomorrow to prepare for your hearing."

Strange, Ruby thought, staring into the shadows. They'd just had the most incredible night of her life, and she suddenly felt more distant from him than she had in weeks.

Had he used her and was now closing himself off from her? She prayed not.

Ruby wasn't sure how long she lay reliving every detail of the past hour in her mind before her eyes drifted shut and sleep finally claimed her.

Chapter Thirty-Three

Lincoln lay completely still, staring up at the canopy top of his bed. Ruby would be going home soon, and he needed to prepare himself for her departure.

He gently pulled his arm free of her sleeping head and slipped from the bed to stand in front of the window.

Ironic that he'd fallen in love with an Atwood. The one family he'd hated his entire life.

Leaning forward, Lincoln pressed his forehead against the cool glass of the window. The hatred he'd grown so accustomed to over the years seemed to have left him the moment Ruby had taken him into her arms. Heck, if he were honest with himself, the minute she'd stepped into his life.

Lincoln no longer despised Agatha or Charles, and somewhere deep inside, he found himself grateful for them. For had it not been for Agatha's curse, he'd have never met her granddaughter, Ruby.

He turned from the window to watch her sleep. How peaceful and beautiful she looked lying in the center of his big bed.

Lincoln shifted his attention to the mirror sitting beside the bed. He would get rid of it in the morning. It would only serve as a reminder of his curse.

Lincoln wanted to remember the last month of his life with Ruby as the Beast. For in the form of the Beast was where he'd learned to love.

And love her, he did. More than he'd ever thought possible.

Emotion choked him to the point he couldn't breathe.

He staggered over to the table the glass-covered rose sat on and gazed at in sorrow. No matter how much he loved Ruby, he couldn't force her to stay. The humane part of Lincoln knew he had to let her go, and the Beast within him submitted.

Opening the drawer on the small table, he pulled out the deed to Ruby's house. With an unsteady hand, he grabbed a pen and signed his name at the bottom, reverting it back to her.

He would call Templeton in the morning and have him move the money that Charles had lost gambling into Ruby's bank account. All six-hundred-fifty-thousand dollars.

Ruby could afford to finish school and become the veterinary doctor she'd started out to be.

Lincoln trailed over to the bed with tears swimming in his eyes and laid the papers on the nightstand where she could find them upon waking.

He bent and softly brushed his lips against her cheek, grabbed his clothes and cloak, and left the room.

Lincoln dressed and made his way downstairs. No sounds could be heard anywhere in the house.

He slipped out unnoticed, strode to the boathouse, and boarded his boat. He would go to the cabin until Ruby and her brother were gone. It would be easier for both of them.

But first, he had a stop to make.

* * * *

Lincoln knelt in front of his parents' tombstones, his heart heavy with grief. It had been years since he'd visited their graves.

He touched his mother's headstone, smiled, and told her everything he could think of about Ruby.

"You would have liked her," he ended, tracing his mother's name embedded in the marble. "No, you would have loved her."

"Father?" he whispered, shifting his attention to his father's grave. "I forgive you."

Jumping to his feet, Lincoln returned to the boat, a kind of closure settling deep in his gut. He'd spent most of his young life searching for his father's approval. Approval that would never come.

Lincoln had accepted at an early age that his father could never love him. No one could, for that matter. But Ruby had shown him a kindness he would hold inside forever. She'd given him a gift he would never be worthy of. And no matter what kind of life he was doomed to live from that moment on, he would always have those memories to cherish.

He drove the boat up the river to the cabin and secured it to the dock.

Gators slipped into the water as he strode up the hill, opened the door, and disappeared inside.

Plucking up a lantern, Lincoln lit it and carried it over to the cot that sat along the opposite wall.

He removed his cloak and crawled beneath the musty-smelling covers, thoughts of Ruby consuming him. He could still smell her amazing scent on his skin.

Lincoln wanted to rail at the empty walls, to strip out of his clothes and dive into the murky river of the Mississippi. Anything to rid himself of the ache that had settled in his heart. But he couldn't bring himself to enter the raging waters. The thought of washing Ruby's scent from his body was unthinkable.

Tossing the covers back, Lincoln surged to his feet and staggered outside to the one place that normally brought him peace, the garden of roses. Yet no peace could be found.

He threw back his head and roared, shattering the silence of the night. "Ruuuuuby!"

Chapter Thirty-Four

Ruby woke to the feeling of something warm and wet swiping against her hand.

She smiled and rolled to her side, blinking against the morning sun. "Linc — "

"Oh," she gasped, her eyes growing huge in her face. "Loki."

The giant wolf sat next to the bed, whining and licking her palm.

"What is it, boy?" Ruby crooned, slowly reaching up to rub between his ears.

He allowed her caress, moving closer and laying his head on the side of the bed.

Ruby glanced toward the bathroom to find it empty and the light turned off.

"Where's Lincoln? Hmmm?" She scratched Loki a minute more, then threw back the covers and got to her feet.

She padded to the bathroom and turned on the shower, listening for sounds of Lincoln.

He must be downstairs, she assumed, stepping under the heated spray.

Her stomach fluttered in excitement at the thought of seeing him again. Would he be down in the dining room, waiting on her to have breakfast?

She finished her shower, quickly dried off, and wrapped a towel around her body on her way to the armoire for clothes.

Papers on the nightstand caught her eye. *Those weren't there the night before.*

Noticing Lincoln's signature at the bottom, Ruby plucked up the papers and began to read.

The more she read, the faster her heart began to pound. Tears filled her eyes and nausea settled in her gut. Lincoln had signed over the deed to her house.

Ruby knew she should be happy about that, but somewhere deep inside, she felt used. Lincoln had slept with her and paid her in full.

He'd succeeded in hurting her after all.

Returning the papers to the nightstand, Ruby took some clothes from the armoire and dressed with jerky movements.

Her cell phone rang from the vanity next to her, displaying an unknown number.

"Hello?" she answered in a wooden voice.

"Miss Atwood? This is Saul Templeton. We met before."

Ruby cleared her throat, hoping to dislodge the lump that had formed there. "Yes. I remember you."

"The reason for my call is to inform you that all monies your father lost gambling at Barone's Gentlemen's Club have been moved to your account. If you have any questions, Mr. Barone has my number."

Ruby paused to gather her voice. "Thank you, Mr. Templeton. I understand everything perfectly."

Disconnecting the call, Ruby slipped on her shoes, tucked her phone into the pocket of her shorts, and descended the stairs.

"Good morning," Mrs. Tuff called out from the dining room. "Are you ready for breakfast?"

Food was the last thing on Ruby's mind at the moment. "Thank you, Mrs. Tuff. Maybe later. Do you know where I can find Linc — Mr. Barone?"

The housekeeper frowned. "I thought he was with you, miss."

"He was gone when I woke up this morning. You haven't seen him at all?"

Mrs. Tuff shook her head. "No, but your brother was awake earlier. He had breakfast out by the pool. Walked a few feet on his crutches."

Excitement pushed out some of Ruby's despondency. "Really? That's great! He's getting stronger by the day. Thank you, Mrs. Tuff. I really needed some good news."

"Well, then I hate to be the one to give you some not so good news, but that hurricane is supposed to make landfall late tomorrow night, and we are definitely in its path."

If not for the impending storm, Ruby would take Cameron home right then and there. She now had enough money to pay for his care. But she wouldn't risk his safety for the sake of her pride.

"I appreciate the update, Mrs. Tuff. I need to make a call and check on my elderly neighbor."

The housekeeper merely smiled and scurried back toward the kitchen.

Ruby dug out her cell and put a call in to Mrs. Fleming on her way to visit Cameron.

When no answer came, Ruby left her a voicemail, telling her to be safe and to batten down the hatches.

Upon entering Cameron's room, she noticed him sitting up in bed watching television. "Cam, you're awake!"

"Hey, Ruby," he greeted, accepting her hug and kiss on the cheek.

Ruby pulled up a chair. "How are you feeling?"

"Good. My leg hurts a little, but I can't wait to be able to get up again."

"You don't want to overdo it," she responded, her gaze landing on a book resting on his nightstand. "Do you remember what happened to you?"

Cameron shook his head. "I was getting Mrs. Fleming some donuts and coffee. That's all I can remember."

Ruby was thankful he couldn't recall the accident. The trauma of it might be too much for his young mind. "I know you're tired of lying in this bed, sleeping all the time. Hopefully, that will change soon."

"It's not so bad. I've just had some weird dreams lately."

"Dreams? Like nightmares?"

Cameron shrugged. "They're not really scary anymore."

"Tell me about them."

Cameron stared straight ahead for long moments as if trying to recall something. "This monster comes into my room late at night."

"Monster? What does this monster look like?"

"I don't know," Cameron admitted in a quiet voice. "I can't see his face behind his hood."

Ruby stilled. "What does this monster do when he visits you?"

Cameron indicated the book on the nightstand. "He sits in that chair you're in and reads to me."

More than a little curious, Ruby leaned over and picked up the book. "Does he talk to you?"

Her brother shook his head. "He only reads to me."

"What makes you think he's a monster, Cam?"

"Because he has claws on his giant hands."

Ruby's heart began to pound. "That doesn't mean he's a monster. Maybe he just needs a manicure?"

Cameron grinned, a hint of his mischievous self shining in his eyes. "That's funny."

Ruby smiled as well, thinking that Lincoln had been to see her brother without her knowledge.

Cameron suddenly grew serious. "This one time while he was reading to me, he looked up, and the light got under his hood. I couldn't see his face, but I saw his eyes. I always thought monster's eyes would be black."

"What color eyes did this monster have?"

"Blue," Cameron answered on a jaw-popping yawn.

Ruby got to her feet and kissed his cheek once more. "Get some rest, Cam. I'll come back and visit you later this evening."

"I love you, Ruby."

"I love you too, Cam."

Leaving the room, Ruby made her way to the kitchen in a daze. Lincoln had been visiting her brother to read to him while she slept. Apparently, there were more layers to the Beast than he allowed people to see. And a much bigger heart, her mind whispered, remembering the gentleness of his touch.

"Are you all right?" Mrs. Tuff questioned, pulling Ruby out of her melancholy.

Ruby wanted to cry and confess that she didn't think she would ever be all right again after finding her payment on the nightstand that morning. Instead she mumbled, "I'm fine."

Chapter Thirty-Five

Ruby exited the cab and trailed up the courthouse steps with more than a little trepidation.

What if the judge didn't feel she was settled enough to legally place Cameron in her care? Any number of things could go wrong this morning.

Ruby pulled the door open and stepped inside a brightly lit lobby.

Security guards stood at a checkpoint while people emptied their pockets and placed their purses on a conveyer belt.

Ruby was no exception. Setting her wallet and phone in a small box, she walked through the magnetic archway and emerged on the other side. "Which way to Juvenile Court?"

The officer pointed her in the right direction.

With a nod of thanks, Ruby strode down the long hallway and nearly ran into Templeton.

"This way." He indicated a waiting area that sat in front a door labeled Courtroom B.

Ruby followed him without delay.

Templeton glanced at her over the rim of his glasses. "You appear nervous. Don't be."

"How can I not be? Some judge who doesn't know my brother or me is about to determine whether Cameron is placed with me or put in foster care. I can't let him go into the system, Templeton. I won't."

The attorney smiled reassuringly. "When we go in there, do not speak unless you are asked a direct question. Understood? Let me do all the talking."

"I understand."

The door abruptly opened and the bailiff waved them forward. "The judge will see you now."

Ruby's legs felt as if they were made of rubber, so great was her anxiety.

She skirted the long table in the room and sat down next to Templeton.

The door opened again, and a well-dressed man strode in with Mrs. Goodson trailing close behind him. They took their seats directly across from Ruby and Templeton.

The proceedings took longer than Ruby would have expected, with the judge taking testimony from both sides.

After an hour of information being passed around, the judge raised his hawkish gaze and addressed Ruby. "Miss Atwood, do you feel that you are capable of taking the best care of your brother? If so, tell me why."

Nausea rolled through Ruby, so scrambled were her nerves. She folded her hands in her lap to slow the trembling and met the judge's all-knowing stare. "Your Honor, I'm not going to give you the flowery speech I had prepared in my mind, because that's not who I really am."

She took a calming breath and continued. "Cameron is my brother, my flesh and blood. I would die for him if it became necessary. I realize that I'm young and lack the experience that someone older might have, but no one else could possibly love him like I do. I have a home for him and plenty of money to see that he has everything he could possibly need."

She paused, holding the judge's gaze. "Please don't take him from me."

Compassion flickered in the judge's eyes before he shifted his gaze in the social worker's direction. "I've read your report, Mrs. Goodson. And frankly, I'm not surprised by it. Your reputation for finding problems where none should be has greatly preceded you this time."

Looking back down at the papers in front of him, the judge picked up a pen and signed several places. "Sole custody of Cameron John Atwood is hereby awarded to his sister, Ruby Atwood."

Tears of elation sprang to Ruby's eyes. She spontaneously hugged Templeton before thanking the judge and sailing from the room.

"I told you there was nothing to worry about," Templeton remarked, strolling along beside her.

Ruby laughed, so happy she could barely contain herself. "You knew he was going to give me custody?"

"Of course. He's married to my sister."

At Ruby's next chuckle, Templeton sobered. "But I will tell you this. If he had truly thought you would not be the best fit for Cameron, it would have turned out differently. Congratulations, Ruby."

"Thank you so much, Templeton. Now, if you'll excuse me, I need to check on my neighbor, Mrs. Fleming, and make sure she has a plan for this hurricane that's supposed to land tonight."

"You be careful," Templeton called as Ruby hurried outside and hailed a cab.

Ten minutes later, Ruby climbed from the cab in front of her house and let herself inside.

She changed into jeans, a red T-shirt, and running shoes.

Packing up a few things for Cameron, Ruby locked up the house and hurried next door to her neighbor's.

She rang the bell.

No answer.

"Ruby?"

Ruby stilled at the sound of Spencer's voice and then slowly turning to face him.

His dark-blond hair sparkled in the sunlight, and his green eyes were hidden behind a pair of sunshades.

Ruby realized something in the moment. No matter how handsome she'd always thought Spencer, he wasn't half the man Lincoln was.

Lincoln was strong and brave, gentle yet tough, with the bluest eyes Ruby had ever seen. So, what if he'd been born a beast. He was *her* beast, and if she had anything to say about it, he always would be.

She marched past Spencer, down the steps. "I have nothing to say to you."

"Well, I have plenty to say to you." He gripped her arm on her way past, halting her on the bottom step.

Ruby yanked free of his hold. "Well, it'll have to wait. I need to get back to Cameron."

"Oh yes," he sneered, following her down to the sidewalk as she hailed another cab. "Back to the Barone mansion. I never thought you'd sell yourself in such a way, Ruby. Especially to that freak. I've heard the stories about him. His deformed face. He eats live animals. Did you know that?"

The crack of Ruby's palm against the side of Spencer's face echoed off the sides of nearby buildings. "Get a life, Spencer! You don't know what you're talking about."

Ruby quickly tossed her bag into the backseat of a cab that had stopped and climbed in after it.

Slamming the door, she gave the driver Lincoln Barone's address.

Chapter Thirty-Six

Lincoln's heart ached. He hadn't seen Ruby in nearly two days. God, but he missed her.

The winds had begun picking up, indicating the storm was drawing near. But he didn't care. Nothing mattered to him but Ruby. And she was probably long gone by now.

A howl rose in his throat, but he swallowed it back. It would do him no good to continue thinking of her. The nights would be torment enough.

One particular night haunted his mind, and would no doubt haunt him for the rest of his life. The night Ruby had surrendered to him.

The pain of never seeing her again nearly doubled him over with its intensity. How was he supposed to go on without her? Never to see her face or hear her laugh again?

He could have kept her with him for a longer amount of time, but she'd have grown to hate him. Of that, he had no doubt.

Ruby was like a bright star in the sky, outshining the millions of others, independent and beautiful.

Lincoln didn't regret letting her go. He only regretted not telling her how much he loved her. *It's better this way. For both of us...*

* * * *

Ruby glanced at the grandfather clock as it began to chime. It was nine o'clock at night, and Lincoln still hadn't returned. "The wind is really picking up, Mrs. Tuff. Where could he be?"

Mrs. Tuff had been wringing her hands for the past several hours. "I don't know, Ruby. He's never left for this long before without telling someone."

A thought suddenly occurred to Ruby. "Where are the keys to the boat?"

"Mr. Barone took the boat," Stiles piped in, glancing at the darkened window by the door.

Ruby followed his gaze, listening to the wind howling outside. "Do you know where I can find another one?"

Stiles paused as if thinking. "My brother-in-law has a little jon boat. He left for Mississippi to ride out the storm."

"Can you go get it for me?" Ruby pleaded, moving to stand next to him at the window.

Stiles paled slightly. "You aren't thinking of going out in this weather, are you? Mr. Barone would kill me if something were to happen to you."

"I doubt that," Ruby responded with a lift of her chin. "Can you get the boat or not?"

Still, Stiles hesitated.

"Please!"

With a sharp nod, he jerked the door open and disappeared into the night.

"Are you really going out in this storm to look for Lincoln?" Mrs. Tuff breathed.

It was the first time Ruby had ever heard her use his first name. "I am. If this storm gets as bad as I think it will, he'll never survive out there."

Mrs. Tuff's eyes grew round. "You don't know the master very well. He can survive anything."

"Why do you call him master?"

The housekeeper shrugged. "It was what Lincoln's father preferred we address him as. I reckon it made him feel better about the boy."

Anger flew through Ruby. "Old man Barone must have been a real piece of work."

"Oh, he was, miss."

Twenty minutes later, Stiles came barreling through the front door, water dripping from his hair. "The boat is tied up down by the boathouse. The rain is coming down harder, Miss Atwood. Are you sure you want to go out there?"

"I'm sure. If I'm not back in an hour, make sure Cameron is safely in the basement."

Mrs. Tuff followed her to the door. "Please be careful out there."

Ruby ran down the hill to the boathouse, large drops of warm rain blurring her vision.

She climbed into the boat, stumbled to the back, and pull-started the motor. It fired up on the second try.

Taking a seat in front of the motor, Ruby steered the boat down the choppy waters of the Mississippi with one destination in mind. The cabin.

A light flashed over the front of the boat, sending Ruby's heart into her throat.

She peered behind her, squinting through the pouring rain into the darkness beyond. But there was no sign of someone following her.

Ruby gave the motor more gas, speeding down the river as fast as the winds would allow.

"Why didn't I grab a flashlight?" she muttered aloud, searching for the dock in the dark.

She slowed her speed and drove the boat closer to the right-side bank.

There's Lincoln's boat, she thought, guiding the vessel up next to his. Ruby tied her boat to his and climbed onto the dock.

With the wind whipping through her hair, she ducked her head and crept in terror along the dock. *Alligators could be anywhere.*

Lightning flashed, illuminating the cabin in front of her.

Ruby had never been more scared yet elated in all her life. Lincoln was only a few feet up the hill.

Gathering her courage, she waited for the next flash of lightning and then ran toward the hill like the hounds of Hell were following her.

She nearly fell over the bottom step in her haste to reach the cabin.

"Lincoln?" she called, pounding on the door.

It abruptly opened, and a cloak-covered Lincoln appeared in the entrance. "Ruby?"

"Thank God I found you! We have to go. The hurricane is about to hit."

"You shouldn't have come here."

A strong gust of wind blew through the area, sending a chair slamming into Ruby's side. She fell off the porch in a tumble of arms and legs.

"Ruby!" Lincoln bounded down after her and had her in his arms before she could suck in a breath.

"Are you all right?" he growled, already moving back toward the porch.

An explosion rent the night, piercing Ruby's eardrums with the deafening sound.

Lincoln jerked forward but didn't drop her.

It took her a moment to realize he'd been shot.

Another ear-piercing sound rang out, sending Lincoln staggering forward once again.

He dropped to his knees with Ruby still in his arms. "Run."

"Nooooo!" Ruby cried as his arms went limp and he toppled over to his side.

Tears spilled from her eyes to mix with the rain slapping against her face.

Ruby scrambled to her knees, her gaze searching the darkness for any sign of movement.

"Leave us alone!" she screamed, hovering over Lincoln's body to protect him as best she could.

When no more shots rang out, Ruby placed her arm behind Lincoln's head and lifted. "Lincoln? Please wake up."

He moaned, his voice raspy from pain. "Get out of here."

"I'm not leaving you," she choked out, lifting his head higher against her chest. "We have to get you to the boat. Do you hear me? You have to help me. I can't carry you."

Another moan slipped past his lips.

He struggled for a minute to get to his knees, the constant lightning showing his hood had come off.

Ruby jumped to her feet, bent, and pulled one of his arms around her neck. "You can do it, Lincoln. Come on."

His great weight nearly took her back down, but she managed to stay upright. Barely.

Lincoln stumbled and staggered alongside Ruby, falling several times on their way to the dock.

The winds had picked up, making it ten times more difficult to walk.

After several minutes of struggling, an exhausted Ruby helped Lincoln into the jon boat. She would have taken Lincoln's, but she doubted the keys were in it.

Covering his face with the hood of his cloak, Ruby pull-started the engine and drove the small vessel through the wind and rain back to the mansion.

Chapter Thirty-Seven

Ruby managed to reach the boathouse without capsizing. She tied the boat to the dock and lifted the edge of Lincoln's hood. "I'm going to go get some help. I'll be right back for you."

When he didn't respond, Ruby lowered her ear to his mouth. No air could be felt.

"Lincoln?" she cried, laying two fingers against his neck. His pulse could barely be felt.

"No. Don't you die on me!"

Scrambling from the boat, Ruby ran against the forceful wind to the side door of the house and jerked it open. "Stiles!"

"Miss Ruby?" Stiles gasped, rounding the corner to the kitchen. "What on earth?"

"Bring help to the boathouse. It's Lincoln. And hurry!"

Without waiting for a response, Ruby ran as fast as her legs would carry her back to the boathouse. She sailed over into the boat and pushed back Lincoln's hood. "Help is on the way. Can you hear me?"

She checked his pulse again, tears of relief and fear dripping down her cheeks.

"Where is he?" Stiles called, barreling into the boathouse with Lincoln's doctor and Mrs. Tuff right on his heels.

Ruby scrambled back to make room for the two men. "He's been shot. Twice!"

Stiles and the doctor managed to heave Lincoln out of the boat and lug his great weight into the house.

Mrs. Tuff ran ahead to get the door.

"Take him up to his room," the doctor wheezed, turning toward the stairs.

Ruby hurried up in front of them, frantic with worry. She sailed into Lincoln's room and yanked the covers back on his bed.

Stiles and the doctor awkwardly placed Lincoln's massive body on the oversized bed.

"Get me my bag," the doctor barked at no one in particular.

Stiles scrambled from the room, nearly tripping on a rug in his mad dash for the door.

"Is he going to be all right?" Ruby whispered as the doctor opened Lincoln's cloak and ripped his shirt down the front.

The doctor spoke without pausing. "I don't know, but I'll do everything I can to save him. I need hot water, alcohol, towels, and plenty of bandages.

"I'll get them," Mrs. Tuff announced from the open doorway she'd just arrived in.

Stiles came rushing back inside holding a black bag in his hand. He quickly set it on the nightstand next to the bed.

The doctor immediately began gathering what tools he needed and started an IV. "He's lost too much blood. Where is that alcohol?"

"Here," Mrs. Tuff gasped, running back into the room with an armful of supplies.

The next two hours seemed to drag by with Ruby pacing along the foot of the bed, tears dripping from her chin.

The hurricane had arrived and brought with it one-hundred-twenty-mile-an-hour winds. But the storm outside paled in comparison to the storm battering Ruby's heart.

Branches slapped against the windows, and the lights began to flicker. What could be taking so long? she wondered for the hundredth time.

"I'm losing him," the doctor suddenly snapped, starting chest compressions.

The room tilted beneath Ruby's feet. Her legs began to shake so hard she could barely stand.

"Lincoln, please!" Ruby cried, crawling up on the other side of the bed next to him. "Please don't leave me."

The old grandfather clock downstairs chimed, announcing the first stroke of midnight. Lincoln's birthday. *Chime.*

"Tell me what to do!" Ruby sobbed.

Lightning cracked, and the lights flickered off and on once again. *Chime.*

Ruby couldn't breathe, so great was the pain in her chest. She couldn't lose Lincoln. Not like this and not on this night. *Chime.*

"Pinch his nose closed, tilt his head back, and breathe into his mouth," the doctor ordered, loading a syringe and injecting it into Lincoln's IV. *Chime.*

"What is that?" Ruby whispered, adjusting Lincoln's head. She pinched his nose closed and closed her mouth over his.

"It's atropine."

The doctor continued with the chest compressions while Ruby breathed every ounce of life and love she had into Lincoln's mouth. And she did love him, she realized, praying for some sign that he still lived. *Chime.*

"I have a pulse," the doctor announced seconds before the lights went out, throwing the room into total darkness.

Ruby lifted her head, tears of relief dripping from her chin. The twelfth chime sounded.

She shifted her gaze toward the table in front of the window as another flash of lightning illuminated the room. The last petal of the rose had fallen.

The room began to vibrate with the thunder of a train. A sonic wave erupted through the air, blowing out the windows in its wake.

Ruby covered her head and leaned over Lincoln's face to protect him from flying glass.

Another sonic wave blew through the room, shattering the mirror that stood against the wall near the head of the bed.

"What was that?" the doctor cried from somewhere in the dark.

Stiles came rushing into the room, a lantern in hand. "What in the world was that?"

Ruby opened her mouth to speak, but the words died on her lips.

The light from the lantern touched on Lincoln's face. His amazingly beautiful face.

"Lincoln?" Ruby whispered, stroking his cheek with trembling fingers.

His eyelids slowly lifted to reveal those electric blue eyes. "Ruby?"

A strangled sound burst from Ruby's throat. She leaned in and brushed her lips across his. "Yes, Lincoln. It's me. You're all right. Everything is okay now."

"You came for me," he whispered weakly. "In a hurricane."

"Yes." Ruby half laughed half cried. "I love you, you big idiot. I would brave the fires of Hell for you."

A suspicious moisture appeared in Lincoln's eyes. "I love you too. God, I love you so much, Ruby."

Ruby kissed him again before he succumbed to sleep once more.

"Bring that light closer," the doctor demanded, already returning to his job of working on Lincoln.

Stiles did as he was told, meeting Ruby's gaze. "Who shot him?"

"I don't know," Ruby confessed, reaching down to take hold of Lincoln's hand. "But I have a good idea."

Chapter Thirty-Eight

Lincoln winced, attempting to sit up in bed.

"You shouldn't be up yet," Ruby scolded, entering the room with a tray in her hand.

She set it on the nightstand. "Besides, I might have wanted to crawl in there and cuddle with you."

Lincoln's chest constricted with emotion. Ruby, beautiful, stubborn Ruby had broken his curse. She loved him. He still couldn't believe she actually loved him.

It had been two days since the hurricane's devastation. Two days since Lincoln had become the man he was meant to be. And a two-day lead for the person who'd shot him.

Ruby held a cup of tea to his lips. "Drink."

Lincoln drank as much as he could stand before indicating he'd had enough. "I'd much rather look at you than drink tea."

"I like looking at you too, my handsome prince."

Handsome. It was still hard to believe that he no longer wore the face of a beast. "You have no idea how much you mean to me."

"Show me," she teased, returning the teacup to the tray.

Taking hold of her hand, Lincoln tugged her forward and covered her soft pink lips with his.

He loved how she sighed into his mouth.

She broke off the kiss and pulled back a little. "Detective Hall called this morning. They arrested Spencer Wright for your shooting."

Lincoln's brows lifted. "What led them to him?"

"Me," Ruby admitted with a shrug. "I told them about his visit here, and how he accosted me outside my house on the day of the hurricane. They got a search warrant and found the weapon in his possession."

Fury burned through Lincoln. His voice came out deadly soft. "He attacked you?"

Ruby shook her head. "No. He just grabbed on to my arm in an attempt to stop me from leaving."

"What did you do?"

"I hit him."

Lincoln's lips twitched. "So, you actually accosted him?"

"It's not funny, Lincoln. He shot you. You nearly died."

He reached up and tenderly touched her cheek. "But I didn't die. I'll never leave you again, Ruby. How's Cameron?"

Ruby smiled. "He's doing so much better. He has Mrs. Tuff wrapped around his pinky finger."

"Good. She needs something more than Stiles."

A giggle escaped Ruby. Lincoln found himself returning her grin.

He suddenly sobered. "I don't want you to go back to the city, Ruby."

Gritting his teeth against the pain, Lincoln reached over and opened the nightstand drawer. He felt around until he found the box he searched for.

Ruby tilted her head. "Lincoln?"

Lincoln slowly opened the box and held it up for Ruby's inspection.

There, tucked inside, lay his mother's diamond engagement ring. "Ruby Atwood, would you do me the honor of being my bride?"

"Yes," Ruby whispered through her tears. "Yes. A thousand times yes."

The sounds of clapping and cheering could be heard outside the door.

"You might as well come in," Lincoln called to the trio now standing in the doorway. He pulled the ring from the box and slid it onto Ruby's finger.

Cameron hobbled over to the bed using his crutches. "You're getting married?"

"Yes," Ruby breathed, holding her hand up to the light.

"So, does that mean we can stay here?" Cameron asked with a little too much excitement.

Lincoln leaned back against the pillows and watched as his staff hugged and welcomed Ruby into the family with open arms.

Mrs. Tuff, of course, hovered close to Cameron in case he needed her.

Stiles winked at Lincoln as if he were a normal man. And Lincoln supposed that he was. Though a part of the Beast would always live inside him, the man he was born to be, lay in that bed, surrounded by the people he cared most about. And Ruby, ah Ruby. She'd stood by him through it all.

What a pair we make, Lincoln thought, nearly choking on emotion. Beauty and the Beast...

Epilogue

Six Years Later

Ruby lay in bed next to her five-year-old son, Lincoln Charles Barone, telling him a story about a beautiful princess who'd fallen in love with a beast.

She loved nighttime stories with Charlie, after his bath when his little body smelled of lotion and innocence.

"Timmy at school says there's no such thing as monsters, Mommy."

"Ah," Ruby whispered, kissing his sweet, soft face. "I never said anything about monsters."

"Well, beasts are monsters."

Ruby smiled over the top of his head. "Not all beasts. Take Loki, for instance. He's not a monster, but he sure is a giant beast."

"Loki's not a beast," Charlie squealed, his little eyes crinkling at the corners.

Lincoln stepped into the room, instantly turning Ruby's insides to mush. If she lived to be a hundred, she'd never grow tired of looking at his handsome face.

"What are you two talking about?" Lincoln whispered, easing his big body onto the bed next to Ruby.

"Mommy says there really are beasts, but Timmy's mom told him there's no such thing."

The corner of Lincoln's mouth lifted. "Really? Timmy's mom said that?"

"Yes." Charlie nodded with an importance that belied his small stature. "She said that's just stuff parents tell kids to scare them."

Lincoln picked up Charlie's hand and kissed his small fingers. "Oh, I don't know, son. Sometimes, when the moon is full and the wind blows just right, I can swear I hear the howl of a lone beast, somewhere in the distance."

"You do?" Charlie's eyes grew as large as quarters.

Ruby sent her husband a wink before meeting her son's gaze. "I think we all have a little beast in us, Charlie... Even you."

* * * *

Lincoln and Ruby went on to have two more children: twin girls. One with chestnut hair and electric blue eyes, the other an exact replica of her beautiful mother.

Ruby eventually finished school and opened an emergency vet clinic in town, becoming one of the most sought-after vets in New Orleans.

Lincoln refurbished the cabin and rose gardens that had belonged to his mother, and gave them to Ruby as an anniversary gift.

It was rumored that Templeton secretly courted Mrs. Fleming, but for some reason that could never be proven.

Cameron went on to college, became a paleoanthropologist, and started a family in his late thirties. He moved into the Atwood home and had two children, both of whom followed in his footsteps.

Stiles and Mrs. Tuff never admitted to their relationship. Although the entire house knew of it.

Spencer Wright was charged with the attempted murder of Lincoln Barone and served ten years in prison. He eventually left Louisiana and moved to Texas where he worked as a bartender until dying of liver failure at fifty-eight-years-old.

Detective Richard Hall eventually uncovered the truth behind Charles Atwood's murder. Apparently, Lincoln Barone hadn't been the only man Charles owed a gambling debt to. For the small sum of eight thousand dollars, Charles Atwood lost his life.

No one ever revealed what happened in Lincoln's room the night of the hurricane. The doctor took Lincoln's secret to his grave, and the staff stayed on until their deaths some thirty years later.

Loki remained a part of the family until the ripe old age of eighteen. Upon his death, Lincoln buried the wolf behind the cabin, next to the garden of roses.

As for Ruby and her Beast? Well, they lived happily ever after…

~The End~

Read below for a sneak peek into the
pages of Enigma: What Lies Beneath –
A Science Fiction Thriller/Romance

Prologue

"Abbie, wait."

Henry's voice could barely be heard over the thundering of waves crashing in the distance.

An endless stream of tears streaked down Abbie's face as great racking sobs seized her small body. Pain welled up from her chest until it became impossible to breathe. Still, she ran.

Her father's shouts faded with every step she took until they disappeared altogether.

Branches grabbed at her arms like the bony fingers of a thousand skeletons, cutting into her skin. She welcomed the sting of every scratch; anything to relieve the pain in her heart.

Her mother's cold, pale face burned behind her eyes, frozen and empty. Gone were the laugh lines, the sparkle...the life.

Abbie couldn't bear to see her mother lying in a box for hundreds of people to pass by and say words over. She might be only seven, but she was old enough to know it meant goodbye. A coffin, they'd called it. Resting place. Final.

A wail wrenched from her small chest. It ricocheted off the trees, scattering birds in different directions. She'd give anything to have wings in that moment, to fly away and never look back.

Abbie burst onto the beach without slowing. Her little legs ate up the sand as she ran straight for the water.

Memories of swimming with her mother lit through her mind in sorrowful detail. The laughter, splashing around and exploring the unknown.

A storm was coming, but she didn't care. She needed to feel her mother's presence, to beg God to give her back.

"Abbie, do you know why the ocean is salty? It's all the tears God cries when someone passes away."

"Mama, what does 'passes away' mean?"

"Well, it means when people die, they leave this earth to become angels."

"If they get to be angels, then why does God cry?"

"For the ones that are left behind who will miss them after they're gone."

Abbie sailed headlong into the waves with her sights on the second sandbar. She would swim out as far as she could to be sure her prayers were heard. If God cried enough to create an ocean, maybe He would take pity on her and give back her mother.

The weight of her skirt wrapping around her legs made it hard to move in the churning water. She used her arms to pull herself along in a rowing motion until the current became too strong, forcing her to dive under and swim. Her eyes stung from the salt, but she held them open while memories of her mother's voice whispered through her mind.

"Abbie, did you know that dolphins can communicate with humans?"

"What is commu... Commu —"

"It means talk to them."

"Have you ever talked to a dolphin?

"I sure have."

"Really? What did he say?"

"He said for me to tell my daughter to stop peeing in the water where his kids play."

Her mother's tinkering laughter echoed through Abbie's heart as she fought the tide in search of the sandbar.

Abbie's arms eventually grew weary and her lungs began to burn, leaving her no choice but to kick her way up for air.

Her head broke the surface to a wall of water high enough to block out the sun. She opened her mouth to scream a second before a powerful wave crashed down on top of her, taking her back under.

Her body spun head over heels along the gulf floor, leaving her powerless to stop the undertow. Panic gripped her as sand scraped her face, entering her mouth and eyes. The need to breathe became too strong, and Abbie gave up the fight. *Pain. Darkness.*

* * * *

Cold. Abbie felt chilled to her bones. Her chest burned, and something was caught in her throat. A spasm gripped her, and she heaved.

A voice she didn't recognize. She screamed for someone to help her, to remove the heaviness from her neck.

Something slid along her arms to her hands.
Tingling warmth. Heat spread out from her
palms through her stomach and legs. The
shivering stopped.

"Salutem." The strange word came from a
deep voice above her. Was she dead?

She slowly lifted her heavy lids and stared
up into the brilliant green gaze of a teenage boy.
His eyes were a color she'd never seen before,
resembling a few of the marbles she'd been
recently collecting.

"God?" she wheezed.

He cocked his head to the side as if he didn't
understand.

She tried to lift her arm, but he held it down.
His hands were covering hers, palm to palm. He
tilted his head to the other side, and more
tingling heat pulsed through her skin. The pain
in her chest receded.

The boy peered down at her in open curiosity, similar to the way she'd seen her dog do when he spotted an insect crawling through the grass.

"Who are you?" Abbie whispered, realizing the boy had saved her life.

He glanced up at something in the distance before returning his gaze to her once again. She wondered if maybe he didn't speak English, and pulled one of her hands free of his to point at herself. "Abbie."

"Abbie," he repeated in a strange accent.

"Yes." She touched her finger to his chest. "And your name?"

Shouts could be heard over the crashing of the waves, and the boy suddenly stilled. Abbie watched in wonder as he sprang away from her and dove into the water.

She pushed up onto her elbows in time to see him swim out toward the sandbar with the speed of a dolphin before disappearing from view altogether.

"No, wait!" she wheezed, rising to her knees at the edge of the gulf. Her gaze flew over every wave of the rolling water, but there was no sign of her savior. Fear gripped her, and she forced herself forward. She had to find him.

"Abbie!" Her father's terrified voice shouted in the distance. "Abbie, sweetheart, don't move! Daddy's coming."

How could the boy stay under the water so long? she wondered, searching the sandbar and beyond for signs of her rescuer.

Henry was suddenly there, scooping her up into his arms. "Somebody call 911."

"Daddy, we have to help him." Abbie tried to wriggle free, but he only held on tighter.

"Help who, sweetie?"

"The boy."

Her father turned in a half circle, scanning the beach without slowing his steps. "What boy?"

"The one who pulled me out of the water."

"There's no one there, honey. And don't ever scare me like that again."

He began to run toward the dunes where a small crowd flocked in their direction with cell phones in hand.

"Is she all right?" an older woman with bright red lipstick yelled as she stumbled along the sand. But Abbie was no longer listening.

She twisted her head around, frantically searching for the boy who had magically disappeared in the great pool of God's tears.

Chapter one

Twenty-five years later

"You really should eat better, young lady. Your mother would have my behind if she were alive to see some of the dreadful things you consume."

Abbie hid a smile at her father's scolding. "I'm thirty-two years old, Henry. I doubt she would go all June Cleaver on me."

"You shouldn't call me Henry, you little brat. It makes me sound old and boring."

"If the toupee fits." They both laughed a moment before falling into a comfortable silence.

Abbie's mother had died from cancer twenty-five years earlier, and Henry had never remarried. He hid his loneliness behind a mask of indifference and immersed himself wholly in his work.

Being the lead epidemiologist for Winchester Industries had become Henry's proverbial crutch, and he spent entirely too much time alone at the lab.

Abbie worried about him constantly and planned evenings such as the one they had tonight to spend quality time together. It didn't always work. She knew he saw her mother every time he looked into his daughter's eyes. The exact replica of the only woman he'd ever loved.

The trill of a phone broke the silence, and her father excused himself to take the call.

Work, no doubt, Abbie thought, taking a bite of the burger she'd just made to her liking.

He reappeared a moment later with a guilty look in his eyes. "That was the lab, honey. They need me to come in."

"What could be so important that it can't wait until morning?"

He avoided her gaze. "I'm not sure, but I'll call you later. Don't wait up. It's going to be a late night."

Something in his voice kicked her curiosity up a notch. He never could hide things well, and the whole no eye contact? Yeah, he was definitely keeping something from her.

"I'll come with you." She pushed her plate aside and stood.

"Nonsense. Stay and eat your heart attack on a bun. You worked a twelve-hour shift at the hospital today."

Abbie had worked at Winchester Industries with her father for several years and often assisted him in the lab before she'd been unceremoniously laid off due to supposed budget cuts.

She knew the higher ups had purposefully kept things from her during her time working in the lab, but whatever Henry hid from her now had to be awfully big for him to outright lie to his only daughter.

And she had no doubt he evaded the truth by the way his left eye twitched. That little trademark had always given him away. "What are you not telling me?"

He pursed his lips. "Okay, you got me. I didn't want to have to say this, honey, but you are adopted."

A chuckle bubbled up before she could stop it. She stood on tiptoes and gave him a quick peck on the chin. "That explains a whole heck of a lot."

"You look so much like your mother, Abbigail. She had the same hazel eyes and dark hair. Her rear end wasn't quite as big though."

Abbie playfully smacked him on the arm before stepping back. "I inherited the infamous booty from you, Henry."

She knew he didn't like her to call him Henry any more than she appreciated him referring to her as Abbigail. They were incorrigible teases, but it was their way.

"I really do have to run, sweetie."

"At least let me pack up your food to take with you, or you won't eat."

He nodded and began gathering his work paraphernalia while she bagged up his dinner.

What are you up to, Henry?

Abbie followed him to the car and held the door open as he deposited his things on the passenger seat.

"You are welcome to stay here tonight, Abbie. Jax would love the company."

"I probably will. If I leave, I'll feed him before I go."

He gave her a two-finger salute and slid behind the wheel.

Abbie stepped back as the door closed and the engine roared to life. He backed out of the drive without another glance in her direction.

She waited until his tail lights disappeared around the corner before going back inside to put food out for Jax. He followed her around with a rubber ball in his mouth, bumping into her legs. The big German shepherd had been with Henry for nearly ten years and had become part of the family.

"You know what's going on, don't you, boy?"

His tail wagged in response from the attention.

"Wanna give me a clue? No? I didn't think so. You are a male after all." She snagged the ball from his jaws and tossed it across the room, grinning as he bounded after it.

After a quick shower, Abbie brushed her teeth and strolled to her old bedroom in search of something to wear. Henry kept the room exactly as Abbie had left it before she'd gone off to college, right down to the blue pom-poms hanging from the bedpost.

She dressed in a pair of jeans and a black tank top, pulled her long dark hair back in a ponytail, and made haste cleaning up the mess from their earlier dinner.

Grabbing her keys, she switched off the lights and left the house.

Abbie marched to her car with determined steps. Something was up, and she wasn't about to remain behind to play the docile daughter while her father was probably neck deep into something illegal.

* * * *

Abbie pulled into the parking lot of Winchester Industries and switched off the engine.

Her father's car sat in its reserved spot in front of a sign that read *H. Sutherland.* She grabbed the registration to her vehicle from the glove box, exited the car, and glanced up at the camera situated on the corner of the building.

Security would be a piece of cake. She did, however, need to figure out a believable reason for being there in the first place without alerting Henry to her presence.

The evening security guard waved from his perch behind a small, less than clean window. Smudges on the glass blurred his smile, but she couldn't mistake the shiny gold tooth displayed so proudly from its position in the front of his mouth.

The door buzzed once, and a *click* told her the lock had released. She pulled it open and stepped inside.

"Hi, Willie. How are you this evening?"

Willie had been one of her favorite night watchmen. His uniform always appeared clean, neatly creased, and he smelled nice. The badge he wore shone perfectly to match the bald spot on top of his head. He had a toothy grin for everyone and a heart of gold.

"Doing good, Miss Abbie. I sure have missed your face around here. The place hasn't been the same since you were laid off."

"Thank you, Willie. I miss you too."

Willie cleared his throat. "What brings you here?"

"Henry forgot an important piece of his work." She held up the folded car registration before quickly tucking it into the pocket of her jeans.

"I hate it when that happens. My wife is always harping at me about how forgetful I'm getting. I reckon she's right. It's hard getting old."

He glanced suspiciously at the pocket she'd tucked the paper into. "He must be working on something pretty big to bring you down here at this hour. It's almost nine o'clock."

Abbie inwardly groaned. She hated lying to Willie, but left with little choice, lying was exactly what she did.

"He's working on some antimicrobial susceptibility tests, and they called him in to straighten out a mix-up in results. It could be the fact that he used the gradient diffusion method instead of—"

Willie laughed, effectively cutting her off. "Okay, Miss Abbie. You lost me back at antimicro…something." He waved her on. "Tell him not to work too hard."

"Have a good night, Willie. Tell that beautiful wife of yours I'm ready for more of her fried chicken."

"I sure will." He beamed.

He touched her arm as she turned to go. "Wait. Dr. Sutherland left his dinner down here when he signed in. Do you want to take it up to him on your way through? If not, I can buzz him and let him know it's here."

Abbie ground her teeth. If Willie picked up the phone, he would spill the beans without realizing it. The man loved to talk.

"Yes, thank you. I'll take it." She caught sight of a keycard peeking out from under some papers on Willie's desk and quickly snagged it when he bent to retrieve Henry's dinner from under the counter. She stuffed the card into her back pocket.

He straightened and handed her the bag. "Here you go, Miss. Abbie."

"See you, Willie." She winked at him and hurried off down the hall.

The cameras strategically placed along the corners of the ceiling made her nervous. If anyone involved in whatever Henry worked on recognized her, they would surely sound the alarm.

Abbie knew Winchester Industries pushed the limits and sometimes experimented with drugs not previously approved by the FDA. But whatever her father had rushed to the lab for had nothing to do with illegal testing. He wouldn't have been asked to come back in for that alone. No, this was definitely something bigger.

To increase her chances of staying under the radar, Abbie bypassed the elevator for the stairs.

Taking them two at a time, she stopped at the door to the second floor. With a slight tug, it cracked open enough that she could see into the hallway. She stood there for several heartbeats, listening for any sound, and then slipped quietly into the corridor.

Male laughter rang out up ahead, and Abbie stilled. *Are they guarding the lab?*

She glanced up at a camera in the corner. Monitors were installed in every office throughout the building, along with the security hub. The longer she stood in the open, the higher her chances were of being seen.

After a moment, the voices grew faint, signaling the men had headed off in the opposite direction. She blew out a breath she'd been holding and crept silently forward.

Noticing the door to the lab was closed when she rounded the corner, she quickly fished out the keycard from her back pocket and slid it effortlessly through the vertical groove situated next to the doorjamb. The green light activated right on cue, and she cringed as a *click* sounded loud enough to startle a sloth.

The predictable sounds of a lab in use met her ears as she eased the door open and entered her father's domain. He obviously hadn't heard the lock disengage over the consistent beeps and humming of the equipment surrounding him.

Abbie took in the room with a quick glance, noticing a big pair of feet hanging off the end of a bed her father stood next to.

Her heart began to pound as she crept farther inside. The closer she got the more confused she became. It was definitely a man lying on the bed; only, she'd never seen one that size in her lifetime.

A sheet covered his lower body from waist to ankles, leaving his upper half bare. His chest appeared devoid of hair and stood off the bed about two feet. He was massive and had to be at least six foot ten by her estimation.

Warmth enveloped Abbie as her gaze slid to the stranger's face. *Beautiful would be a gross understatement.*

He had a smooth, strong jaw that angled up to slightly pointed ears. *Pointed ears?* His dark hair lay haphazardly tousled on the pillow. Full lips and a faintly crooked nose made up the rest of his face. She wondered what color his eyes were.

Without conscious thought, she inched forward on shaky legs. *Why would they have him here? Is he sick? Contagious?* It didn't matter as long as she could stand there and drink him in.

Her father must have sensed her approach. He stiffened a second before spinning around. "What are you doing here?" He seemed more nervous than angry.

"I could ask you the same thing. What's going on, Henry?" She nodded toward the incapacitated stranger taking up far too much bed.

"You have to leave. Now."

Anger surged. "What is that man doing here? This isn't a hospital, so don't lie me. I knew something was going on when you got that phone call earlier. What sort of illegal activity do they have you involved in this time?"

"Honey, please. You're not supposed to be here. You need to go home. Now. I'll explain it all in the morning." He glanced toward to door several times as he spoke.

"Not until you tell me the truth. You promised me you wouldn't participate in anymore illegal activities, Dad. No matter what Newman threatened you with."

Henry took a deep breath and pinned her with an impatient stare. "Fine. But then you must go. And it's not what you think. Newman didn't threaten me, but he might if he finds you here. How did you get in here, anyhow?"

Abbie raised an eyebrow. "Newman's not going to find me here. And Willie let me in. He doesn't know what kind of illegal dealings go on in this lab. He was told that I was laid off due to budget cuts."

Henry averted his gaze. "You're going to be the death of me."

Chapter Two

Abbie stared at her father as he attempted to explain away the man's presence with some fabricated tale.

"This is all I know. It…" Her father took a deep breath and started again. "It washed up on the beach a few hours ago. Newman called me in to run some tests before they extradite the corpse to Area 51."

"Wait." Abbie held up a hand when he would have continued. "Newman called you in? Why would the CEO of Winchester Industries be interested in someone that washed up on the beach? And why are you referring to him as an *it?*"

He hesitated. "It's not human, Abbie. I don't know what it is, but I need to get these samples taken before the crew from Area 51 arrives. You have to go. No one else is to know about this."

"Not human? That's impossible." Other than the stranger's size and pointed ears, he appeared the same as any other man. "And how did he get here?"

Henry turned to a computer near the head of the bed and tapped a few keys. The screen came out of hibernation within seconds to display what looked to be a chest X-ray.

"Someone ran across the thing on the beach. Apparently it drowned somehow and floated up on shore. Local PD had the creature sent to the morgue, and Newman had it delivered here. He told the police this was a Hazmat situation and needed '*him*' contained until they cleared the scene. No one questioned Newman since he owns the hospital and this lab. The cops had no idea it was an alien."

"Why would they think he's not human? Did the coroner open him up and find a little green man in residence?" She would have rolled her eyes if the situation didn't already resemble a *Twilight Zone* episode.

"Come look at this."

Abbie stood next to her father to gaze at the unbelievable evidence of a six-chambered heart. It took a moment to register what she was looking at, but there was no mistaking it.

"How is that possible? I've never seen anything like it. Do you know what this means?" Her voice sounded strained to her own ears.

"Neither have I. And it doesn't mean anything to us. Once it leaves here, we forget it exists."

"But, Henry —"

"No." He glanced at his watch. "The crew will arrive in less than three hours to retrieve it, and then I develop amnesia. Do you understand?"

"We have a little time before they get here. Show me please? This is too amazing to be true." Several questions ran through her mind at once. She couldn't voice them all.

With a click of the mouse, another image appeared. "Do you see that?" Henry pointed to an object on the screen.

"Yes, what is it?" She leaned in to get a better look.

"The equivalent of lungs."

"But what is that?" She indicated something winged that grew from the sides of the organs.

"They're gills." His voice took on an awed tone, which she could understand. She was in the same frame of mind.

"It can't be." The evidence of it mocked her from inches away.

Henry glanced up at her. "They're gills, I tell you. I saw them on the back side of his ribs. His arms cover most of them and they wouldn't be noticeable to someone that didn't know what to look for."

"Do you realize what this implies? Gills for God's sake."

"I'm seeing similarities to humans, amphibians, reptiles, and fish here, Abbie. The heart of a fish only has two chambers, one to receive blood and the other to send it out to the rest of the body. A human heart has four.

"Notice that our blood leaves the lungs and enters the heart, while a fish's blood leaves the heart and enters the gills. And take a gander at this." Henry clicked the mouse once more.

"What in the world?" she breathed, studying the image before her.

"It's the digestive tract. I would give anything to be able to dissect it."

His excitement at the possibility of a dissection disturbed her.

Abbie glanced over at the *it* in question, and something tugged at her emotions. Some kind of beautiful creature had washed up on the beach only to be violated and sent to a place few had ever witnessed. *Area 51.*

She shuddered and turned back to the screen. "Have you ever seen anything like this before? And why six chambers instead of two or four?"

"I don't know why the six chambers. I understand that an octopus, squid, and cuttlefish have three separate hearts, so perhaps it has to do with evolution."

"Or God created him that way," Abbie argued.

Pinching the bridge of his nose, Henry continued. "I studied tissue samples taken from an unknown subject many years ago, but I wasn't told its origin. And it had blood. This subject doesn't. Well, not enough to fill a cup, at any rate. And there are no wounds that it could have bled out from."

"What?" Abbie was sure she hadn't heard him right.

"Come here and I'll show you." Henry took up residence on the left side of the bed as she rushed around to the right.

He lifted the creature's left arm, turning the hand so she could see both sides. "We attempted to draw blood here first. Nothing. Not a drop could be found."

Replacing the arm, he gripped the subject's chin next, tugging it to the side for her inspection. "One vein runs along here, from jaw to the bottom of the neck. Dry also."

"But— "

"I'll come back to that. There's more." He dragged the sheet down to a small pink vertical scar on the creature's abdomen. "Impossible," he gasped.

"What's wrong?" Her gaze flew to her father's face." Henry had significantly paled.

"I made that incision less than an hour ago. It seems to be healing. The thing is dead. I don't understand."

"Are you sure he's…gone?" Abbie couldn't bring herself to refer to him as *it*.

"No heartbeat." Henry laid two fingers on the creature's neck. "No pulse. It's dead all right."

"So how did he heal if he isn't alive?"

"I don't know. I was able to remove a very small sample of something resembling blood from the stomach cavity, but it wasn't in any of the A, B, O, or RH classes. It's an anomaly."

"Perhaps you should try giving him a universal donation to see what happens? I mean, if he healed, he has to be alive."

"He? It's not a person, Abbie. And I'd thought of that. I was just about to try it before you snuck in here and gave me indigestion. I'm running out of time. I want you gone before that crew arrives."

"Then let's hurry. I'll help."

He shot her an impatient glance. "So stubborn."

"Yet another thing I inherited from you."

Henry spun on his heel and left the room.

Abbie took advantage of her father's absence to study the beautiful creature before her. His wrists and ankles were strapped down with leather cuffs attached to bands that disappeared beneath the bed.

He looked very much alive to her, with color in his cheeks and his lips slightly parted. She was certain his mouth had been closed only moments before.

Her fingers shook as she reached toward him. She gently pushed his top lip up with her thumb. "What in the world?" she whispered, jerking her hand back as if burned. He had razor-sharp incisors where his eyeteeth should have been.

When nothing untoward happened, Abbie slowly leaned in again and froze. Heat instantly surrounded her upper body. She felt a soft tugging sensation that left a tingle in its wake. Her muscles relaxed without effort as something unseen moved up the sides of her face.

A deeply accented voice invaded her mind. *"Open."*

Abbie knew she should run, but the allure of the command was more powerful than her fear.

She allowed the warmth to pull her closer, never taking her gaze from his mouth, until she half lay across his massive chest with her arms on either side of his shoulders.

A gentle pressure wrapped itself around her mind, and she found herself inching toward his parted lips to hover slightly above them. His breath mingled with hers, and she breathed him in. *He's breathing?*

Abbie felt as if his very spirit entered her body, traveling down her throat and circling her chest. The pressure continued to slide through her stomach and grew in strength as it reached her legs.

She had no desire to move even if it were possible. Her insides turned to liquid, and she exhaled softly into his mouth only to draw him in again. *He's alive...*

Abbie shifted on his huge frame and stroked her fingertips down to his wrists. Though no pulse was evident, she could feel his energy, his breath teasing her lips.

On instinct, she gripped his hands and slowly turned them over until she was palm to palm with him. A gentle electrical current traveled up her arms, tingling, pulsing, as if it had a life of its own.

An image of herself as a child coming awake on the beach while waves washed over her legs suddenly flashed through her mind, and she jerked her head back. *What is happening?*

The pulsing continued through their points of contact while Abbie held her breath, lowering her face close to his once more. Another jolt entered her palms.

"Salutem."

Where had she heard that before? She recognized it as the Latin word for greetings.

Images and voices began swirling together in a multitude of color and sound, leaving her helpless against the onslaught.

"Abbie, did you know that dolphins can communicate with humans?"

A groan slipped from her parted lips, full of pain and sorrow. *Mother.*

More current slid from his hands to hers. *"Salt from his tears." Water. Coffin. Death.*

*"*No," she softly moaned.

Sand. Her lungs hurt. Heat snaking through her arms and legs. "Salutem." Blessed darkness.

Abbie heard a keening sound and realized it came from her. She slowly removed her shaky hands from his and brought them to his face. "It can't be."

With unsteady fingers, she rested her thumbs on his eyelids and gently lifted. A soft gasp escaped as she stared into the emerald-green eyes of a dream she'd thought long forgotten.

Memory was swift and strong, and she clung to it like a life raft on a raging sea.

She'd wondered a thousand times about the day they'd buried her mother, when the teenage boy with the strange accent and rare-colored eyes had magically appeared to save her life.

The memory had faded over the years until she'd convinced herself it'd all been the imagination of a child who'd recently suffered a trauma.

Abbie couldn't believe the boy from her dreams was actually real and strapped down before her now.

She forced herself to break the connection and stand on legs that felt too weak to hold her up. His warmth abruptly disappeared, leaving an ache and emptiness in its place that was staggering.

Chapter Three

Unimaginable pain. Hauke *could hear his sister's scream piercing the night, ripping his heart in half. Sunlight scorched his skin. The cool, healing power of the water.*

He could breathe once again. Voices. More pain. The distinct feel of a blade opening his skin.

His defenseless state enraged him. To be trapped inside his own mind, unable to retaliate as someone violated his body.

A female. Compassion.

Images plagued him, making little sense.

He clung to the female's voice. She touched him. He knew she attempted to soothe him, yet he couldn't read her thoughts.

"Open," he mentally implored.

Her mind became partially exposed to him as he beckoned her closer. His spirit clawed its way to the surface, craving hers. It was a hunger unlike anything he'd ever known.

Her breath entered his mouth, and he felt as if he'd died a thousand times. He saw her lovely face in its true form behind his closed lids. Soft, warm, and expressive. She cared about what happened to him.

He took in her sweet scent, amazed as his spirit encircled hers, wrapping itself around her life force in a slow, deliberate slide.

The connection broke unexpectedly, and he panicked. The pain from it went beyond the physical to be felt in his very soul.

Something pricked Hauke's arm, and warm, blessed liquid traveled up, straight into his heart. It beat for the first time in hours — days... He was unsure of how long he'd been gone. If not for the membrane in the roof of his mouth producing the enzymes he needed to heal and keep his organs from shutting down, Hauke knew he would already be dead. He had no clue how long he'd been in the coma-induced sleep.

The sensation kept coming, and he realized blood somehow pumped into him. The female had to be responsible, he thought, feeling his body soak up every last drop of the coveted source.

Somewhere inside his subconscious, he knew it to be human blood now coursing through his veins. Forbidden among his kind, yet there was nothing he could do but allow it to happen.

Moisture filled his eyes in stark relief, and his protective lenses slid into place. He lifted his lids enough to see shapes moving around the room.

The female's voice sounded from somewhere near his feet, and he zeroed in on her. She wasn't beautiful in the conventional sense, though still very attractive. Light surrounded her. He wished she would come closer where he could see her eyes.

A beeping noise echoed around him, and someone shouted from nearby. "It's alive, Abbie! Get back."

"I'm okay, Henry. He's strapped down and not fighting."

Abbie...

Hauke's people had been familiar with the English language since the great flood over two thousand years ago. Some of the words had changed over time, but he had little trouble keeping up. Although, the couple in the room with him did have strange accents, he silently admitted.

Hauke didn't recognize the voice to his left and cut his gaze in that direction. A tall man with gray hair, wearing a white garment stared back at him with wide eyes. Hauke growled deep in his throat, registering him as a threat.

Abbie's voice broke through his defensive state. "Hello? Can you understand me?"

He brought his focus back on her, and his chest constricted with emotion. It was her. The young girl that nearly drowned in the gulf all those moons ago.

The foreign feeling did little to slow his curiosity. He openly stared, drinking in her expressive features.

Hauke wanted to communicate with her, but the older man would hear. He sent her a thought instead. *"I comprehend."*

A small intake of air was the only sign that she might have heard him.

He tried again. *"Come."*

She slowly moved forward until she stood next to his head. The fact that she'd gone to the same side as the man wearing white wasn't lost on Hauke. *She is protecting me.* The thought warmed him.

The female had no idea how much power he possessed. The only reason he hadn't broken loose and snapped the old one's neck stood before him now. He didn't want her to fear him.

"*Abbie.*" He liked the sound of her name.

She appeared nervous but didn't run. There was a determined set to her jaw that he found oddly attractive.

"Move back this instant," the gray-haired one demanded from behind her. "If that thing gets loose, you could be killed. And we have no idea what type of diseases it carries."

Abbie spun around. "Just stop it, Henry. He's alive. Does he look like he's trying to break free to you? Have you no heart? We have to do something before they get here. He will die at Area 51."

"It's not our problem, Abbigail. Their crew is already on the way. There's nothing we can do."

Hauke listened to the exchange, understanding enough to know that the one Abbie referred to as Henry planned on sending him somewhere to die.

He could feel his strength returning with the help of the blood now inching through his veins. The hunger for more grew by the second, and his fangs began to throb in time with his pulse.

"I'm disappointed in you, Daddy."

Hauke didn't miss the catch in her voice or the parent reference. *He is her sire.* He filed that piece of information away for a later time. His first priority was to get out of there and find the group that had been with him before the explosion.

His heart ached with the knowledge that his sister might not have survived. If she'd died, he would destroy every last human involved in blowing the oil well that separated Naura from him.

"What do you expect me to do? Take it home with me and set up a college fund for it? Come on, Abbie. Be reasonable. You saw the X-rays. That thing may resemble us to a degree, but that's as far as it goes. Now keep your distance while I check on the incubated samples. It'll be gone soon, and we have no choice but to forget we ever saw it." Henry stalked off, leaving a fuming Abbie to gape at his back.

The door suddenly opened, admitting a short, beefy man wearing dark blue clothing. Something shiny hung from his shirt. He stood there for a moment, leering at Abbie before coming fully into the room. "What are you doing here, Doctor Sutherland?"

It would appear that Abbie was a healer, Hauke noted, watching the man in blue slowly advance forward.

"My father called me to bring him a case of files he'd forgotten."

"I thought you weren't allowed back inside the building. And who is that behind you on the bed?"

Abbie crossed her arms over her chest. "I was laid off, Donald. Not fired. This man is sick. I wouldn't advise you come any closer."

The guy's beady gaze wandered slowly over her body. "It doesn't surprise me that you were dismissed."

"I'd be willing to bet not much does surprise you," Abbie retorted.

Hauke didn't need to open his mind to feel the venom in her words. They fairly dripped with it.

"I think I'll just double check with your father about you being up here. Where is he?" Donald turned toward the door Henry had disappeared through only minutes before.

"You can't go in there, Donald. He's spinning samples at the moment. You'll run the risk of contamination."

Donald stared back at her with traces of suspicion and lust swimming in his eyes. Lust won out in the end.

"Fine. I'll be in the restroom if you need me...for anything." Donald winked at her and sauntered across the room, disappearing behind a row of bottle-filled shelves.

Hauke bit down hard enough that one of his incisors pierced his bottom lip. He would kill the man for his filthy thoughts of Abbie. Hauke didn't need to touch him to read his intentions.

"Abbie." Her name came out in a whisper only to be swallowed up by the insistent noises of the room. He tried again. "Abbie."

She spun around to face him with surprise registering on her face. "You can speak."

He attempted to lift his arm, but the restraints held him back. It would be easy to break free, apprehend her, and escape back to his home. But the thought of frightening her in any way was unacceptable to him.

"Ubi ego sum?"

"I'm sorry. I don't understand?"

Though Latin was commonplace among his people, Hauke spoke many languages. English had been the most difficult to learn due to the backhanded slang most humans used. The need to practice it over the years had been rare since he'd only come in contact with a small handful of them. But he'd learned it all the same.

He cross-referenced words in his mind. "Where am I?"

"You're in a lab. Someone found you on the beach. We thought you were dead." She cleared her throat. "Wh-what… Who are you?"

"I am Hauke. Son of Klause. What means Area 51?"

She averted her eyes. "Are you in pain?"

That would be an understatement. He ached from head to feet. Even his hair seemed to hurt. "No pain."

"You must be thirsty." She darted away before he could answer.

He would have laughed if it wouldn't hurt to do so. Any other time, he'd enjoy teasing her. And there would plenty of times, of that he was certain.

Hauke tested his bonds. *Simple.* They thought to hold him with their straps.

Abbie returned to his side, holding a clear plastic cup. He gave her a questioning look.

"It's just water."

"Something floats inside." He'd never seen its contents before.

She glanced down at the cup, and her lips twitched. "That's ice. It keeps the water cold."

Her voice took on a husky tone as she leaned over him and slid her arm beneath his head. "Here, try it."

Heat and energy radiated from her in the way Hauke imagined the sun would feel on his skin in that moment.

He breathed deep, taking in her essence. Her spirit was strong, and he felt his own rise to the surface, seeking, craving. *Mate.*

A possessive growl rumbled from his chest, and she stilled.

"Do not fear me, Abbie."

"Did I hurt you?"

He only shook his head.

The sincerity in her voice made him want her more. Emotion poured from her in waves. Her concern over his pain touched him in ways he didn't understand.

She lifted his head off the pillow and brought the cup to his mouth. "Small sips."

The cool liquid touched his tongue, and he bit back a groan. Hauke drank slowly to appease her. If she had any idea he was capable of breathing underwater, she'd probably be horrified. No, he rather enjoyed her caring for him.

Abbie removed the drink from his lips and eased her arm out from under his neck. Hauke missed her touch instantly. He watched her set the cup on a side table and busy herself with the tube attached to his arm.

"Thank you, Abbie."

She blushed but didn't say anything.

"Your sire." He nodded toward the other room. "He is concerned for your safety."

"My Sire?" She gifted him with a small smile. "Where do you come from?"

He ignored her question. "What means Area 51?"

Hauke felt her emotions shift. She was like an open book with her expressive features and guileless eyes.

She hesitated. "It's a place where they… um… I have never actually been there." She appeared flustered. "I'm going to get you out of here. "

The sound of footsteps could be heard coming from somewhere in the back. Abbie quickly put space between her and the bed. The anxiety radiating from her was suffocating.

"It's just Henry."

The whispered words did little to slow the growl rising in Hauke's throat. He didn't trust Abbie's father.

Hauke studied the older man as he progressed into the room. He was hiding something, and Hauke wondered how much of it had to do with the prize he had strapped to the bed.

"One of the samples was compromised. I'm going to need another." Henry went to a stainless steel side table and opened the drawer. He withdrew several items, laying them on top.

"What are you doing with that?" The spike in Abbie's adrenaline wasn't lost on Hauke.

"I'm going to sedate– "

"No you're not!" She practically spat the words.

Henry barely spared her a glance as he lifted a vial from his coat pocket and set it beside the other items on the table. He tore open something that appeared to have a miniature blade protruding from one end, and plucked up the small glass bottle in his other hand. After holding them both up to the light, he pierced the vial with the sharp point.

"I won't let you drug him, Henry. Not gonna happen."

Her father raised an eyebrow. "I refuse to go near his mouth unless he is incapacitated. I'm not running the risk of being bitten, and neither are you."

Available on Amazon

Titles by Ditter Kellen

I am Elle -A Psychological Thriller – Book 1

I am Elle: The Sequel – Book 2

The Boy in the Window

A Paranormal Thriller

Where Corn Don't Grow

Psychological Thriller – Coming Soon

Quick Chronicles
An FBI Thriller Series

Oliver Quick: The Hunter Becomes the Hunted

Oliver Quick – Book Two – The Prophet – Releasing soon

Enigma Series
A Science Fiction Romantic Thriller

Enigma: What Lies Beneath

Naura

Vaulcron

Zaureth

Oz

Gryke

Braum

Rykaur

Thrasher

Zyen

Brant

Zaureth Awakened

The Seeker

A Paranormal Romantic Thriller Series

From the Shadows

A Killer is Born

The Rise of Vlad

Torn

A Fallen Angel Romance

Bayou Heat

A Paranormal Romance

The Secret Series – A Romantic Vampire Thriller

Lydia's Secret – Book 1

Midnight Secrets – Book 2

About Ditter

Ditter Kellen is the USA Today Bestselling Author of Mystery/Thriller/Suspense/Crime Fiction Novels. She also dabbles in science fiction and paranormal romantic thrillers. Ditter loves spinning edgy, heart-pounding mysteries that will leave you guessing until the very end. That includes apocalyptic thrillers with a touch of horror, as well as family drama laced with murder and jaw dropping scenes, some might find difficult to read.

Ditter resides in Alabama with her husband and many unique farm animals. She adores French fries and her phone is permanently attached to her ear. You can contact Ditter by email: ditterkellen@outlook.com

Made in the USA
Columbia, SC
06 December 2019